LOOK FOR MORE ACTION AND HUMOR FROM

GORDON KORMAN

THE HYPNOTISTS SERIES

The Hypnotists
Memory Maze
The Dragonfly Effect

THE SWINDLE SERIES

Swindle
Zoobreak
Framed
Showoff
Hideout
Jackpot
Unleashed
Jingle

The Titanic trilogy

The Kidnapped trilogy

The On the Run series

The Dive trilogy

The Everest trilogy

The Island trilogy

Slacker

Radio Fifth Grade

The Toilet Paper Tigers

The Chicken Doesn't Skate

This Can't Be Happening at Macdonald Hall!

W9-CBR-751

RESTART

RESTART

GORDON KORMAN

SCHOLASTIC PRESS

Copyright © 2017 by Gordon Korman

All rights reserved. Published by Scholastic Press, an imprint of Scholastic Inc., *Publishers since 1920.* SCHOLASTIC, SCHOLASTIC PRESS, and associated logos are trademarks and/or registered trademarks of Scholastic Inc.

The publisher does not have any control over and does not assume any responsibility for author or third-party websites or their content.

No part of this publication may be reproduced, stored in a retrieval system, or transmitted in any form or by any means, electronic, mechanical, photocopying, recording, or otherwise, without written permission of the publisher. For information regarding permission, write to Scholastic Inc., Attention: Permissions Department, 557 Broadway, New York, NY 10012.

This book is a work of fiction. Names, characters, places, and incidents are either the product of the author's imagination or are used fictitiously, and any resemblance to actual persons, living or dead, business establishments, events, or locales is entirely coincidental.

Library of Congress Cataloging-in-Publication Data available

ISBN 978-1-338-05377-7

10 9 8 7 18 19 20 21

Printed in the U.S.A. 23
First edition, June 2017

Book design by Mary Claire Cruz

FOR LEVELS TEEN CENTER
AT GREAT NECK PUBLIC LIBRARY

RESTART

CHAPTER ONE

CHASE AMBROSE

I remember falling.

At least I think I do. Or maybe that's just because I know I fell.

The grass is far away—until it isn't anymore. Somebody screams.

Wait—it's me.

I brace for impact, but it never comes. Instead, everything just *stops.* The sun goes out. The world around me disappears. I'm being shut down like a machine.

Does this mean I'm dead?

Blank.

The light is harsh, fluorescent, painful. I squeeze my eyes shut, but I can't keep it out. It's an explosion.

Voices are babbling all around me. You can't mistake the excitement.

"He's awake—"

"Get the doctor—"

"They said he'd never—"

"Oh, Chase—"

"Doctor!"

I try to make out who's there, but the light is killing me. I thrash around, blinking wildly. Everything hurts, especially my neck and left shoulder. Blurry images come into focus. People, standing and sitting in chairs. I'm lying down, a sheet over me—white, which makes the brightness even worse. I raise my hands to cover my face and suddenly I'm tangled in wires and tubing. A clip on my finger is tethered to a beeping machine next to my bed. An IV bag hangs from a pole above it.

"Thank God!" The lady beside me is choked with emotion. I can see her better now—long brown hair, dark-rimmed glasses. "When we found you, lying there—"

That's all she can manage before she breaks down crying. A much younger guy puts an arm around her.

A white-coated doctor bursts into the room. "Welcome back, Chase!" he exclaims, picking up a chart on a clipboard at the foot of my bed. "How do you feel?"

How do I feel? Like I've been punched and kicked over every inch of my body. But that's not the worst part. How am I supposed to feel when nothing makes sense?

"Where am I?" I demand. "Why am I in a hospital? Who are these people?"

The lady with the glasses gasps.

"Chase, honey," she says in a nervous voice. "It's me. Mom."

Mom. Doesn't she think I know my own mother?

"I've never seen you before in my life," I bluster. "My mother is—my mother is—"

That's when it happens. I reach back for an image of Mom and come up totally empty.

Ditto Dad or home or friends or school or *anything*.

It's the craziest feeling. I remember how to remember, but when I actually try to *do* it, I'm a blank. I'm like a computer with its hard drive wiped clean. You can reboot it and the operating system works fine. But when you look for a document or file to open, nothing's there.

Not even my own name.

"Am I—Chase?" I ask.

While my other questions sent murmurs of shock around my hospital bed, this one is greeted with silent resignation.

My eyes fall on the chart in the doctor's hands. On the back of the clipboard is written AMBROSE, CHASE.

Who am I?

"A mirror!" I exclaim. "Somebody give me a mirror!"

"Perhaps you're not ready for that," the doctor says in a soothing tone.

The last thing I'm in the mood for is to be soothed. "A mirror!" I snap.

The lady who calls herself Mom fumbles inside her pocketbook and hands me a makeup compact.

I open it up, blow away the loose powder, and stare at my reflection.

A stranger stares back at me.

Amnesia. That's what Dr. Cooperman says I have. Acute retrograde amnesia—the loss of all memory prior to a certain event. In this case, me taking a swan dive off the roof of our house.

"I know what amnesia is," I tell him. "So how come I remember a random word like that, but I can't remember my own name? Or my own family? Or why I was climbing on the roof?"

"That I can answer," supplies the younger guy, who turns out to be my older brother, Johnny, a college student home for the summer. "Your room has that dormer window. You just open it up and crawl out onto the eaves. You've been doing it as long as I can remember."

"And did anybody warn me I might break my neck?"

"Only since you were six," my mother puts in. "I figured if you survived this long it was time to stop worrying. You were such an athlete . . ." Her voice trails off.

"Amnesia can be an unpredictable thing," the doctor informs us. "Especially with a traumatic injury like this one. We're just starting to understand which parts of the brain control which life functions, but for all we know, it has nothing to do with geography. Some patients lose long-term memory, some lose short-term memory. Others lose the ability to transfer from short- to long-term. In your case, the damage seems totally confined to your sense of who you are and what's happened in your life up until this point."

"Lucky me," I say bitterly.

Cooperman raises an eyebrow. "Don't knock it. You remember more than you realize. You can walk and talk and swallow and go to the bathroom. How'd you like to have to relearn everything, even how to put one foot in front of the other?"

The bathroom part is definitely an upgrade. They say I was in a coma for four days before I woke up. I can't say how the bathroom side of things was taken care of during that time, but I'm pretty sure I had nothing to do with it. Maybe I'm better off not knowing.

The doctor checks a few readings on my monitor, making notes on my chart, and then regards me intently. "Are you absolutely certain you can't remember anything at all from your life before you regained consciousness?"

Once again, I peer back into the nothingness that's where my memory is supposed to be. It's like reaching into a pocket for something that should be there but isn't. Only that something isn't keys or a phone; it's your whole life. It's bewildering and frustrating and terrifying at the same time.

Try harder, I push myself. *You didn't just whoosh into being when you came out of that coma. You're in there somewhere.*

A vague image starts to form, so I bear down, concentrating with all my might, trying to wrestle it into focus.

"What is it?" Johnny asks breathlessly.

At last the details sharpen into view. I see a little girl, maybe four years old, wearing a blue dress with white lace. She seems to be standing in some kind of garden—at least, she's surrounded by greenery.

"Well, there's this girl—" I begin, struggling to keep the picture in my head.

"Girl?" Cooperman turns to my mother. "Does Chase have a girlfriend?"

"I don't think so," Mom replies.

"It isn't like that," I insist. "This is a little kid."

"Helene?" my mother asks.

The name means nothing to me. "Who's Helene?"

"Dad's kid," Johnny supplies. "Our half sister."

Dad. Sister. I search for a connection between these words and the memories they should trigger. My mind is a black hole. There might be a lot in there, but it can't get out.

"Are the two of them close?" Cooperman inquires.

Mom makes a face. "Doctor, after the accident, my ex-husband came to shout and accuse and punch the emergency room wall. Have you seen him here since then, while his son lay in a coma? That should give you an idea of the relationship between my boys and their father and his new family."

"I don't know any Helene," I volunteer. "But you can't go by me because I don't know *anybody*. This is just a little blond girl in a blue dress with white lace. Kind of dressed up, like maybe she's going to church or something. But why I remember her and nothing else, I can't tell you."

"Definitely not Helene," Mom concludes. "She has dark hair like her mother."

I turn to the doctor. "Am I just crazy?"

"Of course not," he replies. "In fact, this little blond girl suggests that your memory isn't gone at all. It's only your ability to access it that's been damaged. I believe that your missing life will come back to you—or at least some of it will. This girl might be the key. I want you to keep thinking about her—who she is, and why she's so important that you remember her when everything else has disappeared."

I honestly try, but there are too many other things going on. Now that I'm not dead, the hospital is suddenly in a big hurry to get me out of there. Dr. Cooperman runs tests on every part of me except my left earlobe. Turns out my brain may be short-circuited but the rest of me still works.

"So how come I ache all over?"

"Muscular" is his diagnosis. "From the fall. Or should I say"—he chuckles at his own joke—"the sudden stop at the bottom. Every muscle from nose to toes tenses up from that kind of shock. Tack on ninety-six hours of complete inactivity, and you stiffen all over. It's normal. It'll pass."

My only real injuries are a concussion and a separated left shoulder. Turns out my bad diving form saved my life. My shoulder hit the ground a split second before my head, absorbing just enough of my hard landing to keep the impact from killing me.

Mom brings clothes for me to change into. I suppose I shouldn't be so blown away that they fit. They're *my* clothes, after all—but of course, they're new to me. I can't help wondering if I have a favorite shirt, or a super-broken-in pair of jeans.

I don't remember the car either—a Chevy van. Or the house. I take the opportunity to fill in a few blanks about myself. I am not the child of millionaires. I have no great love of cutting the grass. Or maybe that one's on Johnny. I've got an excuse: I've been in a coma.

I note the window I must have climbed out of, since it's the only one with roof access. For some reason, I expected it to be higher, and I'm embarrassed. Like it's an insult to my manliness that such a puny fall scrambled my brains.

When Mom opens the door, a chorus of voices cry out, *"Surprise!"*

A makeshift banner hangs across the living room: WELCOME HOME, CHAMP!

A heavyset man about Mom's age steps forward, enfolds me in a crushing bear hug, and rubs his knuckles up and down my head. "Good to have you back, son!"

Mom is horrified. "Stop it, Frank! He has a *concussion*!"

The man—my father?—lets me go, but he's defiant. "Ambrose men can take a few licks, Tina. You're talking about an all-county running back."

"*Ex*-all-county running back, Dad," Johnny amends. "You heard the doctor—Chase can't play football this season."

"Dopey doctor," my father snorts. "What does he weigh? One-forty, soaking wet?" He faces Mom. "Don't turn him into a wimp like you did with Johnny."

"Thanks, that means a lot," my brother says drily.

"Why are you here, Frank?" My mother is quickly losing patience. "How many times have I asked you not to use your key anymore? This is not your house, and it hasn't been for a long while."

"I pay the mortgage on this place," he growls. All at once, the cloud lifts from his face, and he's grinning. "Besides, we had to be here to welcome home the conquering hero."

"Falling off a roof doesn't make me a hero," I mumble. I can't put my finger on it, but there's something about my dad that makes me nervous. It isn't physical. In fact, for a middle-aged guy, he's pretty energetic and spry, despite the paunch and the thinning hair. His smile is totally overpowering. To see him is to want to like him. Maybe that's the problem, I decide. He's too confident that he's welcome everywhere. And going by Mom, he isn't. Not here, anyway.

He's brought his new family—a wife named Corinne, who doesn't look much older than Johnny, and Helene, my four-year-old half sister. Mom was right—Helene's definitely not the girl in the blue dress. It's no big deal, I guess, but I'm disappointed. I was kind of hoping for one thing in my life to be connected to reality.

Although I'm meeting them for the first time, I have to remind myself they already know me. For some reason, they don't seem to like me very much. Corinne hangs back, and the little kid stays firmly attached to her mom's skirt. They look at me like I'm a time bomb about to go off in their faces. What did I ever do to them?

My father seems to be settling in for a long visit, but Mom's having none of that. "He has to rest, Frank," she says. "Doctor's orders."

"What—he's chopping wood? He's resting."

"Alone," she insists. "In his room. Where it's quiet."

He sighs. "Ants at a picnic, that's what you are." He hugs me again, squeezing slightly less this time. "Great to have you back, Champ. Sorry it couldn't be more of a celebration, but

Nurse Killjoy over there—" He inclines his head in my mother's direction.

I stick up for her a little. "She's right about the doctor. He said I have to take it easy because of my concussion."

"Concussion," he snorts. "When I played football, I got my conk bonked plenty of times. You rub a little dirt on it and you're good."

Corinne appears at her husband's elbow. "We're so glad you're okay, Chase. Come on, Frank. Let's go."

I feel like I have to fill the hostile silence that follows. So I lean down to my kid sister. "That's a nice doll you've got there. What's her name?"

She shrinks back like I'm about to eat her.

Eventually, Dad's gone, taking Corinne and Helene with him. Johnny goes out to meet some friends and Mom orders me upstairs to get a head start on the relaxation that almost caused a civil war.

She has to show me which room is mine, because I don't remember any of it—not the wooden staircase with the faded floral runner up the center, not the narrow hallway with the low ceiling, not the wooden door with the crack down the center panel.

My mother sees me evaluating the damage and is momentarily surprised by my surprise. Then she tries to explain it away. "That's probably my fault. I always let you and your friends play sports in the house. You're too big for that now—or the house is too small."

"Which sports?" I ask.

Tears are coming to her eyes. This is hard for her.

"Football. Soccer. Badminton. You name it."

Being in my room is the weirdest experience of all. It's *my* room—there's no question about that. The walls are covered with newspaper clippings about football teams I starred on and lacrosse games I won. That's me in the pictures, diving into end zones and being mobbed by ecstatic teammates—more unfamiliar faces. There are trophies too—shelves of them. *Chase Ambrose, Top Scorer*; *Chase Ambrose, MVP*; *Most Yards From Scrimmage*; *Team Captain*; *State Champions* . . . I'm really somebody!

I only wish I knew who.

It takes some doing to build up my courage, but I eventually make it over to the window. I was wrong before; it's plenty high. I'm lucky to be alive.

It's like I've been parachuted into the middle of someone else's life—someone who looks exactly like me, yet isn't me.

The doctor is right. I need to rest.

I sit down on the edge of the bed—my bed. There's a phone on the nightstand, the screen cracked. I wonder if I had it with me when I fell.

I press the home button. It's dead.

There's a charging cable right beside it, and I plug it in. After a couple of minutes, the display lights up, and there I am again, with two other kids—complete strangers, although you can tell from the pose that the three of us are close friends.

It's a selfie, with the kid on my right as photographer. I'm in the middle, and the smallest of the three of us, which is surprising, since I'm a pretty big guy. It must be Halloween, because there are little kids in costume in the background. I'm wielding a baseball bat, holding it high. Hanging off the tip of it is a mangled, ruined jack-o'-lantern.

The screen goes dark, and I press the button again. The image of the triumphant pumpkin-bashers reappears. I can't take my eyes off it. All three of us wear wild, gleeful, unholy cake-eating grins.

What kind of person am I?

CHAPTER TWO

SHOSHANNA WEBER

Shosh466: Hey, little bro! Wanna smile?

JWPianoMan: ???

Shosh466: Alpha Rat took a header off his roof and almost killed himself.

JWPianoMan: By "almost," you mean . . .

Shosh466: Sorry, still alive, but supposedly messed up. Just got out of the hospital yesterday.

JWPianoMan: Any chance Beta and Gamma Rats fell with him?

Shosh466: Nope, solo performance. Don't get greedy . . . Smiling yet?

JWPianoMan: Now who's being greedy?

I exit messages and call Joel because I'm worried about him. I always worry about him. He's my younger brother—fourteen minutes younger, anyway. But if the thought of Chase Ambrose falling off his stupid roof onto his stupid head doesn't bring a smile to Joel's lips, then something is seriously wrong.

Besides the usual, I mean.

"Hey," he answers.

Even in that single syllable I can pick up the discouraged tone in his voice. He's angry and homesick, and who can blame him? It's not like going away to boarding school was his first choice. Or even his twentieth.

"Is Melton getting any better?" I ask, almost afraid to hear the answer. That's Melton Prep and Musical Conservatory in New Britain, Connecticut.

"What can I tell you? It's exile."

I don't argue with him. How can I? Joel's a talented musician who belongs in a place like Melton. But that doesn't change the fact that he'd still be at home starting eighth grade at Hiawassee if it weren't for what happened.

"How are the other kids?"

"Okay," he replies without much enthusiasm. "All losers, just like me. I'm probably not going to get picked on, if that's what you mean. There are no pickers here, only pickees."

That bugs me. "You're not losers. You're there because you're *winners*. You have *talent*."

"There's a reason why I can't live in my own town, and it has nothing to do with playing the piano. It's Alpha Rat, and you know it. If he fell off a skyscraper instead of his own roof, I'd be on my way home right now."

I have to let that pass, because it's the bitter truth. Chase Ambrose and his two disgusting friends hounded my poor brother out of town. The thought of it amazes me even though I saw it happen. I still can't figure it out. Chase isn't Darth Vader or Voldemort; he doesn't have the Force or dark magical powers. And yet he, Aaron Hakimian, and Bear Bratsky made

Joel's life so miserable that my parents had no choice but to find him a school in another town.

We tried to fight it. My dad spent so much time in the principal's office that it would have made sense for him to leave a change of clothes there. But nothing could be done about the bullying. Most of the time, there was no way to prove who was doing it. A random foot tripping Joel up in a crowded hall, a shoulder rammed into his chest that sent him sprawling—"Sorry, man. Didn't see you." Dog poop pushed in through the vents of his locker, his clothes mysteriously disappearing from the changing room to be replaced by a rabbit suit. When a science project wound up smashed, or a painting ruined in the art room, it was always Joel's. On the night of the talent show, when the fire alarm was pulled, it was during Joel's piano performance.

It started with just Chase, Aaron, and Bear. Eventually, though, it spread. The other kids—well, they couldn't help but notice that every time someone was making a fuss or protesting, stuffed into a locker or mummified with toilet paper, it was my brother. Before you knew it, Joel was the school victim and the school joke. His life was practically unbearable.

Who do you blame? The principal? Dr. Fitzwallace did what he could, but most of the time there wasn't any evidence. Sure, he could make the occasional try. There was this time Chase chucked a lacrosse stick at Joel's bike and the butt end got jammed in the spokes. Joel went flying over the handlebars and wound up with a sprained wrist, a black eye, and a nasty scrape along his jaw stretching from chin to ear. There were plenty of witnesses to that one.

Dr. Fitzwallace was all set to throw the book at Chase—a long suspension, the works. The school board overruled him. They agreed it was wrong to throw the stick, but insisted that Chase couldn't have predicted it would result in serious injury. Ha! The real reason was that Chase was the town sports hero—and the son of the *last* town sports hero. Chase's dad had a lot of admirers on that board. And my family didn't.

The only time anyone was able to pin something on those three idiots, it had less to do with my poor brother than the fact that it cost the district money. At the big open house in May, Joel was invited to play piano. He's by far the best musician around here, even if none of the other kids appreciate it. Anyway, Chase, Aaron, and Bear planted six cherry bombs inside the school's baby grand, timed for the middle of the performance. I can still hear Joel's scream when the big firecrackers went off, splintering the wood of the piano. I think that's part of what makes him such an irresistible target for the Chases of the world—they know they can always get a reaction out of him. After that, Joel couldn't even walk down a hall without a bunch of football players making fun of how scared he was. We were *all* scared, but it's only Joel they remember.

The irony is that the case against Chase and company had nothing to do with the attack on my brother. No—it was the damage to the *piano* that got the administration upset enough to bring in the police. The juvenile court judge sentenced Chase, Aaron, and Bear to community service at our town's senior citizens' home. (As if the elderly deserved that.)

You'd think Chase would leave Joel alone after that. It

would've made sense. But sense has never been an Alpha Rat quality. So my parents found a new place for Joel—because as long as that bully was around, my brother would never be safe.

Joel's probably right that if Chase had fallen off a skyscraper instead of just a roof, he'd be able to leave Melton and come home. Sometimes I feel like I should be up on that tall building, pushing Chase over the side.

But that would make me no better than him. And I am better.

Everybody is.

The night before the first day of school, my dad always used to take Joel and me to Heaven on Ice, which is one of those self-serve frozen yogurt places. Even though Joel and I are twins, our dessert strategies are totally opposite. I get vanilla yogurt with just a handful of chocolate sprinkles. Joel prefers a thimbleful of yogurt and ninety-nine percent toppings. It's a competition to see who can load up the most weight.

I don't want to go this year.

"Come on, Shosh," my dad wheedles. "It's a tradition. All your friends will be there."

"Not my *best* friend."

He gives me a sad smile. "So you and Joel are best friends now? When he's home, you two fight like cats and dogs."

"He should be home *now*." I know Dad's trying to help, but I'm determined to be miserable.

"We've been over this a million times. This is the best thing for Joel. Whatever the reason he's there, he'll learn to love Melton for the music program."

In the end, I let him talk me into going. Mom and Dad are worried enough about my brother. I don't need them stressing over me too.

It's weird to be at Heaven on Ice without Joel. I see Hugo and Mauricia, and the first question they ask is how Joel's doing. The way they say it, it's like he's been shipped off to the moon, not Connecticut. I don't want to deal with the whole sob story again, so I change the subject and ask them about camp—they both went to sleepaway this summer. Right when Hugo is telling me about his life-and-death struggle with a pup tent, I spot . . . *him.*

The jerk.

The worst person in the world.

Chase has a few small cuts and bruises on his face, although nothing like what I was hoping for. His left arm is in a sling, but that's about it. He's standing in front of the row of yogurt dispensers with a timid look on his face like he honestly can't decide what flavor he wants. Isn't that classic? The kid who feasted on Joel—chewed him up and spit him out—can't make up his mind between strawberry banana and rum raisin. Too bad they don't have poison.

He must feel me glaring at him because he glances up and catches my eye.

He looks right through me at first, which is insulting enough. And then he does something so horrible that I can barely believe it, even from the likes of him. He casts me a shy smile.

All the anger that's been building inside me since Joel left for Melton rises to the surface like magma.

Before I have a chance to think about it and stop myself, I stalk over to Chase. I get right in his face and tell him, "You've got some nerve grinning at me after what you did! You stay out of my way or you'll be sorry!"

I take my beautiful vanilla yogurt with chocolate sprinkles, dump it over his head, and sweep out of the store.

My father's in conversation with one of the other dads and almost misses me storming past. "Done so soon?" he asks. Then he looks back inside and sees our family's archenemy, dripping frozen yogurt and sprinkles all down his face, dabbing at himself with a soaked napkin in his one free hand. "Car's around the corner," Dad mumbles, hurrying me away from Heaven on Ice. He's embarrassed, sure. But maybe also a little bit proud.

And how do I feel? I thought there was nothing Chase could do to make me madder at him than I already am. Now I stand corrected. Every time I think about it, my blood boils a little bit hotter.

After all the bad history that went down between him and Joel, I swear he looked at me like he'd never seen me before in his life.

Like he hadn't played a starring role in destroying my family.

CHAPTER THREE

CHASE AMBROSE

I recognize the school. Not because I remember it. It's just that Mom drove me by here a few times over the last couple of weeks to make sure I'd be sort of familiar with the place. It's called Hiawassee Middle School, and it turns out I'm the star of just about every team they have. Or *ex*-star. Until further notice, I'm on the disabled list.

I get this information from my mother on the drive to my first day of eighth grade. It's just the two of us now, since Johnny's back at college. Mom's trying to fill me in on my former life so I won't be caught by surprise, like when that psycho girl dumped frozen yogurt on my head.

Funny—she was sympathetic when I told her about that, but she didn't seem very surprised. Like we live in a town where people attack each other with desserts all the time.

"Oh," she replied airily, "young girls can be oversensitive, especially with a popular athlete. She smiles at you; you don't smile back; she takes it personally—"

"But I *did* smile. She's the one who didn't. She went straight for the yogurt—"

She rolled her eyes. "What do you want me to say, honey? I don't even know who this mystery yogurt bomber is."

But here's the thing: I think she *did* know—or at least she could make a pretty good guess. Why would she hold that back? It wasn't like those first days out of the hospital when she was a stranger to me, and I must have seemed plenty unfamiliar to her.

Now, as we pull to the curb in front of the school, she's pumping me up with details like names of friends and teachers I get along with. Yet I still can't shake the impression that there's something being left unsaid.

"But . . ." I prompt.

She reddens. "But what?"

I put it to her: "Tell me the part you're leaving out."

"Thirteen years is a long time, Chase. There's no way I can fill all that empty space for you while we're parked at the side of the road on the first day of school. You're going to hear things about yourself—good and bad—that might surprise you. Just keep your cool, okay?"

Now, what's that supposed to mean? I asked; she answered. And now I know even less than before.

Her face is the color of an overripe tomato. I don't push it. I'll find out soon enough.

There are hundreds of kids pouring in the front entrance. Everybody seems to know everybody else. Backslaps and high fives fly everywhere. Several of them fly in my direction, and I smack hands, bump fists, and try to look like I belong, which I definitely don't. I also get some strange looks, and a few kids meet my eyes and then furtively look away. I'm guessing this has something to do with the scrape on my face and my immobilized arm and shoulder. Mom warned me that a lot of people probably heard about my accident, but nobody knows the amnesia part. I have to get ready to explain that to a lot of friends who can't figure out why I don't recognize them. The teachers and office staff had to be told, of course.

"It's our *boy*!"

A single bellow rises above the general chatter as soon as I enter the building. I don't know the kid, but I'm willing to bet he's one of my football buddies, judging by the size of him. From out of the hubbub of the foyer, guys who are almost as big are converging on me, slapping at me and calling me their boy.

"Guys—guys! Not the shoulder!" My mind is reeling. How am I going to explain to this welcoming crowd that I haven't got the faintest idea who any of them are? I start to feel a little dizzy.

"Chase!" Two more football players elbow their way to my side. To my surprise, I actually recognize this pair. They're the guys from the pumpkin-smashing picture on my phone. Mom pointed them out in my lacrosse team photo as Aaron and Bear. Apparently, they're my best friends.

"Dude, good to have you back!" barks Aaron, the taller of the two. In person, he has the closest thing to a full beard I've ever seen on a middle-schooler. "We tried to come by, but your mom said you were on bed rest."

"Yeah, I can't believe you're here," chimes in one of the other guys. "Didn't you jump off the clock tower on the village green?"

Bear whaps him hard across the face. "He jumped off his

roof, moron. If he jumped off the clock tower, he'd be dead. And he didn't jump; he *fell.*"

"Who'd be stupid enough to *jump* off a roof?" Aaron adds.

"This was pretty stupid too," I admit, a little taken aback by that full-face smash, and the fact that the kid on the receiving end didn't seem to mind it. "I can't remember what I was thinking. In fact, you guys, to be honest—"

The slappee cuts me off. "But you're going to be healed up in time for football season, right? You'll be ready for our first game?"

"The doctor says no. It's my shoulder, but mostly it's the concussion. I can't risk taking a head shot so soon after the accident."

A howl of protest greets this announcement.

"But we need you!"

"You're our leading scorer!"

"The best player!"

"Our captain!"

"Cut it out, you guys," Aaron orders. "Injuries are a part of the game. We all know that." To me, he adds, "Listen, man. We have to talk to you."

He heads out of the foyer to an inner atrium with hallways leading off it. We have no problem navigating the dense crowd. My two best friends just push people out of the way. Most kids see the three of us and clear out on their own.

They lead me to a bench along the wall.

"Are these seats taken?" I ask a youngish boy, maybe a sixth grader.

Before he can answer, Bear rumbles, "They are now!" The kid scrambles down the hall, propelled by a hefty shove.

I sit down with my fellow pumpkin-smashers. Before they can say anything, I burst out with, "Aaron—Bear—" The names are unfamiliar on my tongue, like I've never spoken them before. "I've got something to tell you. When I fell off that roof, I got more than a concussion and a sprained shoulder. I got amnesia too."

Bear frowns. "Amnesia? You mean you forget stuff?"

I shake my head sadly. "Worse. I forgot *everything.* Like, my whole life before I fell." I motion around us. "The school. These people. All new to me. I wouldn't even know you guys except your pictures are on my phone. As it is, I don't remember anything about us. I know we're friends because my mother said so. But everything we did together—that's gone."

I catch them eyeing each other like they don't believe me. It makes me mad until I consider how I'd react if a longtime friend told me the same thing. Here I am, the kid they've known all their lives. I look the same, talk the same. And I'm telling them that all our history is completely wiped out.

I don't blame them for thinking I'm joking. It *is* a joke. Just not a funny one.

I speak again. "It's not just you guys. Think how it feels to see some random stranger instead of your own mother. Your brother. Your dad. And trust me, I'm not loving the thought of dealing with eight hundred kids in this school who think I'm dissing them because I can't remember who they are."

Bear stares at me hard. "Wait—you're not kidding, are you?"

"I wish," I say fervently.

He's stunned. "Wow."

Aaron leans forward, practically into my face. "Yeah, but your memory's going to come back, right?" There's an urgency in his voice—he must really hate it that I'm missing out on the good old days.

"Some of it. Maybe," I reply. "But also maybe not. The doctor says it's impossible to know."

They look at each other again, and there's no mistaking how freaked out they are. I feel a surge of warmth toward these two—my best friends. I have a giddy vision of my phone screen—the three of us brandishing the baseball bat with the ruined jack-o'-lantern. The good times.

"Guys." I try to reason with them. "I'm still me, even if I don't remember the stuff we did together. We'll do new stuff. Better stuff."

"Oh, yeah, totally!" Bear exclaims. "And if you can't play football, you'll be good for lacrosse in the spring, right?"

"The doctor said I should be okay by then, although we'll have to see—"

"There you go!" He sounds upbeat, although I'm pretty sure he's faking it. This can't be an easy thing to process. If I wasn't the one with amnesia, I don't know if I could accept it myself.

"We're here for you, man," Aaron adds, slapping my back and sending a jolt of fire through my separated shoulder. I swallow an angry warning. One step at a time . . .

"Welcome back, boys," a deep voice intones.

A tall man in a charcoal-gray suit approaches our bench. "Chase, I'm Dr. Fitzwallace, your principal. I thought I'd reintroduce myself, under the circumstances. We've met before, of course."

A strangled "You can say that again" comes from Bear. The principal silences him with a single look through steel-rimmed glasses.

"Chase, come with me. Let's have a little chat."

My friends are already slouching off down the hall, so I follow the principal into his office. On the wall are two large framed photographs, and I'm surprised when I identify one of them. It's on my wall too—part of a newspaper clipping about our football championship last year. It's me, helmet pushed onto the back of my head, hoisting the trophy. The other is similar, although you can tell it's a lot older. The pose is almost identical—a young player raising the same trophy. I can't explain it, but the kid looks sort of familiar. But that's crazy. How can I recognize him? I don't recognize anybody.

Dr. Fitzwallace is watching me. "That's your father. Our only other win at state, back when he was your age."

Wow, no wonder Dad calls me Champ. I should call him Champ too.

I tell the principal, "I didn't know he won at state. I mean, I'm sure I knew at some point—"

"That's exactly what I'd like to talk to you about. Have a seat, Chase." Dr. Fitzwallace waves me into a chair. "I have to confess this is a first for me. I've never had a student suffer amnesia before. It must be very upsetting for you. Even a little frightening."

"It's pretty weird," I admit. "Not remembering anybody. It's like I'm surrounded by all these people, but I'm still alone."

The principal sits down behind his desk. "I hope we can make this situation a little easier on you. I've alerted all the teachers and support staff. So we're ready for you. If you have any issues, just have whoever's involved get in touch with me."

I thank him because that's what he seems to expect me to do.

"One more thing." He leans back in his chair, and when he speaks again, it's slowly and carefully, as if he's trying to get his words exactly right. "This is an awful thing that's happened to you, but it's also presenting you with a rare opportunity. You have the chance to rebuild yourself from the ground up, to make a completely fresh start. Don't squander it! I'm sure you're not feeling very lucky, but there are millions of people who'd give anything to stand where you stand right now—in front of a completely blank canvas."

I stare back at my principal. What is he talking about? I'm struggling to discover the person I was and he wants me to *change*?

What was so wrong about the old me that now I have to be somebody else?

CHAPTER FOUR

BRENDAN ESPINOZA

"The impressive breadth and diversity of wildlife in the modern middle school is on display nowhere more than in the lunchroom. Here we see the species Cheerleaderus maximus *grazing in her native habitat, the salad bar . . ."*

I focus on Brittany Vandervelde and Latisha Butz as they make their delicate selection of lettuce, cucumber, and tomato slices. As I shoot, I balance the flip-cam on my forearm to keep it steady. Everything looks better on YouTube when the camera work isn't all jumpy.

"A longing glance in the direction of the pizza table," I continue my narration. *"But, alas, it is not to be. For* Cheerleaderus, *this meal is garnished with a radish rose and fat-free dressing. And wait—"* I pull back the shot to include Jordan McDaniel, heading out of the food line with a heavily laden tray. *"Could it be? Yes! A rare* Clumsius falldownus, *weaving his way to the nearest table. You can do it,* Clumsius*—Uh-oh, there goes the soup. And that orange, rolling across the floor . . ."* Oh, man, this stuff writes itself. Who needs a script when you've got real life?

"And now we leave the relative safety of the food line and venture into the lions' den," I go on, panning over to the corner table where Aaron Hakimian, Bear Bratsky, and some of their

football buddies are eating too much and laughing too loud. *"This is the land of the carnivores, where lesser animals fear to tread."* Don't I know it! I'm filming on maximum zoom, even though it's bound to be a little blurry. I sure don't intend to go any closer and get fed my own video camera. *"But where's their leader? The apex predator? Could that be him paying for a pack of Fig Newtons at the cash register? Yes, it is—the king of beasts,* Footballus herois, *his thunderous footsteps striking terror in the hearts of all creatures great and small. Watch him make his majestic way to—"*

As I pan my flip-cam to follow Chase Ambrose's path to his football buddies, he disappears from the frame. I frown. He's not going over there. He's headed to somewhere else. I get him back into the shot and struggle to continue my voice-over. *"But wait—mighty* Footballus *has changed direction. He's taking his mighty self to a different table. For reasons known only to his supreme mightiness, he's coming—"*

Oh my God, he's coming here!

I whip the camera away fast enough to leave a trail of burnt air hanging in the cafeteria. He's right opposite me, larger than life, holding his tray over my table.

Why is Chase Ambrose coming anywhere near lowly me? Does he know I'm making fun of him and his friends in a YouTube video?

If so, I'm dead—no *ifs*, *ands*, or *buts*.

My last interaction with him was the time he and his co-Neanderthals stood me against a tetherball pole and then played an intense game, the rope whipping around me until I was trussed up like a turkey. I'd probably still be there if the sanitation workers hadn't come to empty the Dumpster that day. Actually, I'm lucky I wasn't *in* the Dumpster. Those jerks bullied Joel Weber so badly that his folks finally sent him to boarding school.

"Is anyone sitting here?" Chase asks.

I glance up, expecting to get a face full of something. He's standing there, looking like he's never laid eyes on me before. My mind screams, *Red alert! Red alert!* But aloud I say, "Help yourself."

He takes a seat and then actually *spreads his napkin across his lap*! Just like a civilized person! Although—I look down at my own lap—no napkin. And probably none on any lap in the entire cafeteria.

This is the weirdest thing that's ever happened. Unless—

Could the rumors be true? It was the biggest news in town that the great Chase Ambrose fell off his roof and landed on his head this summer. You can still see the cuts and scrapes on his face, and his arm's in a sling. But the gossip around school is that the guy actually has *amnesia*. He doesn't remember anything from before the accident. I thought it was just a rumor . . . but what other explanation could there be for why he's sitting here with me instead of with his football friends? And acting like a human being, no less?

My video on hold, I turn back to eating—and let me tell you, that's not easy when you're sitting across from the apex predator, amnesia or not. I read that some amnesia is temporary. If it all comes back to him, I could have my entire egg salad sandwich shoved up my nose just for daring to be near him. Then I notice that he's struggling to saw away at a barbecued chicken breast. The dull plastic utensils don't make it easy, especially with one arm immobilized against his chest. He's really working hard at it. Beads of sweat stand out on his brow.

I speak the craziest, most foolhardy words that have ever come out of my mouth: "You need help with that?"

"No, thanks." He keeps on sawing, getting nowhere, his frustration growing.

I still can't explain why I do it. I get up, loop around the long table, and approach Chase from behind. "It's easier when both arms work."

He battles a moment longer and then gives in with a sigh. "Maybe I could use a hand."

So there I am in the middle of the cafeteria, hunched over the apex predator, cutting up his chicken. At one point, Shoshanna Weber passes by and shoots me a look that perfectly combines shock, amazement, and disapproval. Or maybe she's just trying to figure why I'm sawing at his meat instead of his carotid artery.

I finish, put down the knife, and hand him back the fork.

"Thanks," he says sheepishly.

"No big deal." I return to my side of the table, sit down—

And hit the floor hard.

A chorus of raucous laughter explodes all around me. That's when I notice I'm surrounded by football players. Bear puts my chair down on top of me, trapping me under it.

"Chase, man, you're at the wrong table," Aaron exclaims. "Come with us. We saved you a spot." They practically kidnap him and drag him to the lions' den.

A few seconds later, the chair is lifted off me, and somebody hauls me to my feet.

Chase.

"Sorry," he says, looking uncomfortable.

"Come on, man! Over here!" comes a volley of shouts.

He hesitates.

"They're your teammates and your best friends," I tell him, because maybe he doesn't remember.

"Right."

If I didn't know better, I'd think he wasn't that thrilled with the idea.

Back in my seat, I take out my camera and realize that the video has been running the whole time. There's no picture, obviously, but the audio is all there.

I might listen to it later just to prove to myself that I've had a close encounter with Chase Ambrose and lived to tell the tale.

CHAPTER FIVE

CHASE AMBROSE

Every time I see a little girl, it brings me back to the one from my memory—the blond girl with the blue dress trimmed with white lace.

I'm not sure why that is. Maybe when you only remember one thing, it sticks with you. If only I could remember where I remember her *from*.

I think of her again when I see the little kid on the monkey bars at the playground. It's my first day without the sling in more than a month—and since forever, in a way, because I remember nothing from before the accident. I'm out walking, enjoying my freedom from the tight wrapping on my shoulder. It feels fine—*normal*—and I need that after two weeks of school that were anything but. Normal is the last word to describe a place where you're a stranger in a strange land despite the fact that everybody knows you.

That's when I recognize the girl scrambling all over the jungle gym. It's Helene, my half sister. She's definitely high-energy, and really kind of cute, crawling through tunnels, whizzing down slides, and just as quickly climbing up again. She's a little too wild, especially up top—I guess she's too young to understand that falling on your head runs in our family.

Just as the thought crosses my mind, she loses her grip and tumbles off the top of the twisty slide. I'm there like a shot, catching her and swinging her around like it's part of the game. She squeals in exhilaration, spreading her arms, and I get into the spirit, making airplane noises.

She's loving it. I'm doubly thrilled because my shoulder is holding up fine. The two of us are having a great time—until she looks down and sees who's got her.

"Mommy!" Her scream carries all around the park.

"It's okay, Helene! It's me! Chase—your brother!"

"I want to go down!" Now she's red in the face and crying.

I set her on the ground and watch as she runs off to join Corinne, who's hustling our way. Great. Dad's family already has a problem with me, and now they're going to think I've been terrorizing their daughter.

"Sorry," I mumble. "I didn't mean to scare her."

"I saw what happened. Thank you for catching her."

There's nothing wrong with what she's saying. It's the way she says it—too polite, too distant, like I'm a stranger instead of her stepson.

Helene has her face buried in her mother's sweater and refuses to look at me.

"I guess she doesn't like me very much," I comment.

Corinne softens. "She's just a little afraid of you."

"Afraid of me?" What could I have done that would make a four-year-old freak out every time I come near her?

Before I can finish the thought, a loud horn honks. A panel

truck pulls up to the curb. AMBROSE ELECTRIC is stenciled on the side.

The driver's side window rolls down and my dad sticks his head out. "Fire up the grill at five thirty, Cor! I'm bringing home the biggest steaks you've ever seen!" He catches sight of me. "Hey, Champ, what're you doing here? You're supposed to be at practice."

I wave. "Doctor's orders, remember?"

"Your arm's fine!"

"Yeah, pretty good." I point to my head. "It's the concussion."

He looks disgusted. "Doctors! They'll keep you in bubble wrap the rest of your life if you let them. Well, how about dinner, then? I'll bet you could use a good steak. You're not going to get your strength back on the rabbit food Mom's slinging at you."

"Thanks. Some other time." I hesitate. "I saw your state championship picture on the principal's wall. I didn't know. I mean, I knew at some point, but—"

He laughs with delight. "There are a lot of athletes out there. But only a few of us can make it rain. There's something special about Ambrose men, Champ. Don't let your mother coddle it out of you like she did with your brother."

He drives off, his truck backfiring as he pulls away from the curb.

"Bye, Daddy!" calls Helene.

"Bye, Helene," I say to her.

As soon as we make eye contact, she looks away.

I'm definitely famous at Hiawassee Middle. The part I can't figure out is whether I'm famous *good* or famous *bad*.

The athletic program is my home here—or at least it was before I got hurt. All my friends seem to be jocks, mostly football players. I guess they were pretty worried when they heard about my accident. I pick up on the occasional grumbling that I have to miss the season. But mostly, people are just relieved that I'm okay.

The Hiawassee Hurricanes are kind of the kings of the school. It's a pretty good role to come out of a coma and fall straight into. Since I'm the former captain, I'm almost like the king of kings. To be honest, though, it's hard to picture how I got along with them so well. They're loud, kind of obnoxious, and even though they're really tight, they spend a lot of time shoving and punching each other. Insults constantly fly between them. They probably don't mean it, but it can get pretty ugly. Was I like that too, when I was—you know—me? Did I greet my closest friends by pointing out imaginary stains on their shirts so I could slap their faces? Did I insult their moms, their grandmothers, and their grandmothers' grandmothers? Probably. Even so, that was then and this is now. I've lost a step, maybe because of my concussion. I can't keep up with those guys anymore.

Aaron and Bear shield me from the worst of it. "Dudes," they'll say. "Dial it down. Our boy's injured." Or they'll step in front of me to absorb a friendly punch or forearm smash. I appreciate their help. Still, it doesn't change the fact that I'm not the Chase I used to be. I almost wish they'd stop trying to protect me. I hate being weak; the other guys are treating me like I'm strong. I'm not—I get that. But maybe I can fake it until my strength comes back.

In the end, Aaron and Bear stress me out more than any of the others, because they ask me all these questions: What do you remember? Is your memory coming back yet? When does the doctor say that could happen? When will you be your old self again?

Since I've got nothing else to offer them, I describe the one memory that I do have—the little girl in the blue dress. They listen with great concentration.

"And?" Aaron prompts, eyes wide.

"That's it. That's the only thing I remember."

"But who is she?" Bear persists. "Where did you see her?"

I shrug. "I don't know. That's all I've got."

They stare at me for a long moment and then both burst out laughing.

I'm annoyed. "It's not funny! Don't you think I'd tell you more if I had more to tell? Do you know what the word *amnesia* means?"

"Relax." Aaron puts an arm around my shoulders. "We've got your back. Boys to the end!"

Aside from the football players, most of the kids act kind of odd around me. Conversations end when I enter a room. Faces turn toward lockers as I make my way down a hall. I get that the whole school's heard the story of my amnesia and they're a little weirded out by me. But that doesn't explain everything. This one girl who's pushing a rolling cart of textbooks—when she sees me walking next to her, her eyes just about pop out of her head. She spins away and slams into the wall of a doorway alcove. Books go flying in all directions. She trips on one and starts to go down, so I grab her arm just to steady her. Then she really loses it.

"Don't!" she squeals so loudly that we're the instant center of attention.

I'm mystified. "Let me help you pick up those—"

"No!" And she's gone, practically running along the corridor, dropping even more books as she escapes.

What did I do?

I ask Aaron and Bear about it after school, and they treat it like the stupidest question ever.

"What do you care if a bunch of random nobodies don't like you?" Bear demands.

"It's not that," I tell them. "She was—*scared*. Where did that come from?"

The two exchange a glance. "Man, you really did lose your memory," Aaron comments.

"Come on, guys. Talk to me!"

Bear is impatient. "We don't have time."

"Why?" I query. "There's no practice today."

"We've got to be at the Graybeard Motel by three thirty."

"What's the Graybeard Motel?"

"We've still got two months left on our community

service," Bear supplies. "At the assisted living place on Portland Street, helping out with the geezers and the grandmas. Not everybody's lucky enough to fall off a roof and get excused."

"I'm on community service?" I may not remember much, but I know that community service isn't like getting a detention at school. It's something you get ordered to do. In court. By a judge.

I struggle to sound casual. The last thing I want to do is come across like a wimp to my two best friends. "What did we do to get *sentenced*"—I nearly choke on the word—"to community service?"

"It was no big deal," Aaron scoffs. "We planted a couple of cherry bombs in the piano at open house. It was awesome! Cops are such sticklers about property damage. Like there's a great piano shortage in the world."

"So we got"—I'm nonchalant, but it takes some doing—*"arrested?"*

"We have to go," Bear insists.

"Yeah." Aaron faces me. "Listen, man, I know it bugs you that you can't remember anything about yourself before the accident. Let me fill in some of the details. Our boy Chase isn't the kind of kid to get bent out of shape about a bunch of idiots overreacting to a few firecrackers. We did what we did, and we got in trouble for it. End of story."

"End of story," I echo. I'm speaking carefully, almost as if I'm trying it on for size. "I mean, nobody got hurt, so what's the big deal?"

Bear snickers. "Yeah, right. Nobody."

"The problem with Hiawassee," Aaron goes on, "is that everybody's jealous of us. I don't blame them. We do what we want, and nobody messes with us. Even the adults are jealous, because when they were kids, they were probably losers too. So when Fitzwallace or some judge gets a chance to slap us down, they go hard, since it's the only revenge they're ever going to get. You can't take it personally."

I nod in agreement. "It's kind of not fair."

Bear grins. "Sometimes I cry myself to sleep at night just thinking of the injustice of it all."

I laugh. Aaron and Bear wouldn't cry if you jammed flaming bamboo under their fingernails. They're the toughest guys in the world.

"Thanks for being straight with me," I tell them—and mean it. "My own mother kept me in the dark about this. I don't know what she's thinking—maybe that if I can't remember it, it never happened."

Aaron shrugs. "It's a mom thing. They're all the same. If it's fun, it must be bad."

"My dad warned me about that," I admit. "He said I shouldn't let her coddle me."

"Your dad is the *man*!" Bear exclaims. "He was part of the best football team ever to come out of this place. Next to ours, I mean. When you come back, we're going to *wreck*!"

That pulls me up short. Bear knows as well as anybody that I'm out for the season. It makes me wonder: Should I be? Dad doesn't think so. It's Mom the coddler who took Dr. Cooperman's word for it.

How much should I put my trust in her? She's the one who tried to hide a pretty major part of my past from me. If it wasn't for Aaron and Bear, I might never have figured it out.

Who knows what else she's holding back?

When Mom gets home from work that day, I'm there at the front door to throw it in her face. "Where do you get off?"

She looks totally bewildered. I forge on. "You were so devastated when I got amnesia—but not too devastated to pass up a little editing job on my life!"

"Editing job?"

"Don't you think I have the right to know that Aaron, Bear, and I were arrested and sentenced to community service?"

She doesn't answer right away. She sets down her bag, shrugs out of her jacket, walks to the living room, and collapses wearily into a chair. At last, she says, "You've just been through an awful ordeal. How can it help your recovery if I tell you a lot of things that are just going to upset you?"

"Thing*s*?" I echo. "You mean there are more? How many other nice little stories have you been keeping away from me?"

She seems genuinely sad. "I'll love you and support you through the end of the world—you know that. I've always seen the good in you, Chase, and I believe that's the person you really are, deep down. But you've had your moments."

I have a sickening vision of faces turning away from me, of

kids shrinking back at my approach, fear in their body language. I think of that crazy girl who was angry enough to dump a tub of frozen yogurt over my head. What if she wasn't crazy at all? What if I deserved it?

Then I think back to the conversation with Aaron and Bear. There are two sides to every story, and Mom is taking the opposite one. But that shouldn't surprise me—her kid got in trouble. *Major* trouble, if the community service is any indication.

"Okay, it wasn't a very nice thing to do," I admit. "But I don't understand why the school had to make such a big deal out of it."

She stares at me. "How can you of all people say that after everything that's happened?"

"Maybe because I don't *remember* everything that's happened!" I shoot back. "They were firecrackers, not grenades! It was a *prank*!"

My mother's expression becomes hard. "Never mind the poor musician you practically put into cardiac arrest. The problem was the auditorium of people that thought they were under attack. It was pure luck that nobody got injured in the panic. I'm sure that's what Dr. Fitzwallace was thinking when he decided to bring in the police."

I hear Mom tell the story and feel ashamed. But if you go by Aaron and Bear, it was a nothing gag that the school blew out of proportion because they were out to get us. Who's telling the truth? Is Mom making it sound worse to scare me straight, because—as Dad says—she's coddling me?

When I got amnesia, I lost thirteen years of myself. I have to replace those memories using what I can pick up from other people. But everyone has a slightly different version of me—Mom, Dad, my friends, the kids at school, even frozen yogurt girl. For all I know, the lunch ladies know me better than anyone else.

Who should I believe?

CHAPTER SIX

BRENDAN ESPINOZA

"A prophet is not without honor, but in his own country, and among his own kin, and in his own house"—that's a quote from the Bible, King James Version.

It turns out this applies to YouTubers as well. Here I am, ready to shoot the greatest video in the history of humanity, and I can't get anybody to help me.

"Come on, you guys," I plead with my fellow vidiots—members of Hiawassee Middle School's video club. "You can't *all* have dentist appointments. It's against the laws of probability!"

"All right, you got me," admits Hugo Verberg, raising his hands in surrender. "I don't have a dentist appointment. The reason I won't help you is because you're completely out of your mind!"

"What do you care?" I shoot back. "That's my problem, not yours. I'm not asking you to do the hard part. I just need someone to be my wingman. Shoshanna—you'll help me, right?"

"Not in a million years," is her reply. "You're going to get yourself in trouble."

"I'll put your name on YouTube as a coproducer," I wheedle.

"Oh, good," she drawls. "It'll help the cops spell my name right when we get arrested. I'm out, Brendan, and you'd be out too, if you had any sense."

So it's no. No from Hugo, no from Shoshanna, no from Barton, no from the whole video club. Mauricia even suggests that I should see a mental health professional.

I slump against my locker, watching them walk away, deserting me. Where's the loyalty? Where's the club spirit? Where's the fire of creativity? The betrayal stings, but mostly, I hate to miss out on this idea. It could be the next thing that goes viral. But it can't go viral if it never gets made.

I look around the crowded hall—kids loading up backpacks for dismissal. Do I know anybody? Actually, I know just about everybody, but none of them will meet my eyes. I'm not the most popular guy at school. I'm not sure why. I'm on the honor roll, president of the video club, champion of the Academic Decathlon two years running. Come to think of it, those are probably some of the reasons why kids aren't lining up to ask what I'm doing after school today. Nobody even acknowledges my existence.

Then, out of the passing parade, someone notices me hunkered down beside my locker. Oh, man, it's Chase! That's all I need to put the finishing touch on this perfect afternoon. Bad enough I can't shoot my video. I don't need to hang by the waistband of my underwear off a peg in the girls' changing room.

He pauses, frowning at me, as if trying to come up with where he remembers me from. It must be weird to walk around your own school knowing nobody when you should know everybody. A familiar face—even mine—must really stand out.

"The cafeteria," I supply. "We almost had lunch together. I'm Brendan."

His face relaxes into a sheepish smile of recognition. His arm sling is gone, and even his cuts and scrapes are fading. "Chase," he introduces himself.

I have to laugh. "Everybody knows you." How can I forget the face that starred in so many of my nightmares? With Joel Weber gone, I might be next on the list of preferred targets. I should have told him my name was Harold. Too late now.

On the other hand, the word is Chase is off the football team, thanks to his head injury. And he certainly seems different than he was last year. Maybe that's because once you've cut a guy's chicken for him, he can never really be that scary again.

So I try the impossible. "Hey, Chase, are you busy this afternoon?"

He shrugs. "What have you got in mind?"

I push my luck. "I'm shooting this video to put up on YouTube, but I need a wingman. Can you help me out?"

Part of me is screaming, *Abort! Abort!* It's one thing to coexist in a world with people like Chase Ambrose. It's quite another to recruit the guy for something nobody else will touch.

He never actually says yes. He just goes with me. I explain on the way. And when I tell him how the video is going to go, he doesn't even tell me I'm nuts. He just laughs and asks me if I'm kidding.

"Just because something is funny doesn't mean you treat it like a joke," I assure him. "Comedy is serious business. If people are going to laugh at this, it'll be because we worked hard at it and got it right."

He actually seems to think that over. "Yeah, I can see that. But I'm not the one who's going in, right? My doctor would freak out—not to mention my mom."

Wow, Chase Ambrose has a mom! I always thought the popular people floated down to earth in a column of pure light from the Great Space Ark.

"It's all me," I promise. "You just have to work camera two."

We stop by my place to pick up the tricycle. Chase even takes it for a test drive on the street, practically cackling with mirth. I laugh too, because he looks pretty funny. He's a tall guy, so as he pedals, his knees rise up around his ears.

My mother comes out to investigate the ruckus. When she sees who I'm with, she's practically ready to dial 911. I can't really blame her. When the Chases of the world hang out with me, it usually means I'm about to be dangled by my feet out a high, high window.

"It's fine, Mom," I soothe her. "Chase is helping me on a video project."

"Good to meet you," Chase introduces himself politely.

She's tight-lipped. "Oh, we've met."

I get Chase out of there before Mom says something I'll regret. We head downtown, taking turns alternately riding, pulling, and carrying the trike. Our destination: The Shiny Bumper car wash on Bell Street.

I hand him the school flip-cam and he goes off to distract the attendants. Chase is even better for this than one of the vidiots, because he's kind of a celebrity around town—not just a star athlete, but the son of the last star athlete. Plus, everybody's heard about his accident over the summer, so all the attention is on him. That leaves me free to sneak around the back and put on the headband with the other camera mounted on it—a waterproof GoPro I brought from home.

Sneaking ahead of the next car, I place the tricycle on the conveyor, bracing my wheels against the tire block that moves vehicles through the washing tunnel. Then I sit down on the trike, reach up to the camera, and hit record. My heart is pounding, and I'm tense with anticipation.

This is it. The moment of truth.

The conveyor pushes me and the first blast of water hits. It's all I can do to keep from screaming. It's ice-cold. Considering the research and planning I did to get ready for this stunt, it never occurred to me that they'd use cold water in a car wash. I take *hot* showers—why wouldn't cars?

The frigid blast has my heart beating so fast it's practically popping out the top of my head. I try to tell myself to get used to it, but it's not possible. I'm hyperventilating to the point where I can't get any air in. Just when I'm about to pass out and topple off the trike, the water stops. Gasping for breath, I glance over to the observation area. Sure enough, there's Chase, filming. I experience a surge of relief. The only thing worse than going through this would be going through this for nothing.

My reprieve is short-lived. The soap is next, pelting down on me like wet snow. They only know two temperatures in here—cold and colder. Two gigantic spinning brushes come at me on robotic arms. I'm vaguely aware that my glasses are gone. That's not important, though. I reach up and confirm that the GoPro is still strapped to my head. Out of the corner of my eye—which stings now, from the suds—I see that Chase is still following along. He's hysterical with laughter, but the camera's steady in his hands, and that's the main thing.

The rinse cycle is next—more hyperventilating—followed by a blast of wind that threatens to hurl me off the tricycle. Actually, it's great. It's the dryer, and it's hot. Even better, it means I'm coming to the end. There should be light at the end of the tunnel, but I can't make out much. I lost my glasses when the brushes did their thing.

When the door lifts, I pedal out of there, nearly running over Chase. He never stops filming, not even when the manager turns off the machinery and comes to chew us out.

"Very stupid, Ambrose!" he yells. "Is this your idea of a joke? You could have gotten him killed, you know. This isn't the first time you've put people in danger in this town. I'm surprised you didn't have a few cherry bombs left over. I'm calling the cops."

"It isn't Chase's fault," I manage to croak. "It's mine." I have very little strength left, but I have to speak up. "The whole thing was my idea. It's my video project. I talked Chase into helping me."

"Brendan?" The manager squints at me. I guess I'm not that easy to recognize, soaking wet and half dead, and my skin all slimy—I think I got a wax treatment in there somewhere. "Is that you? Why would you do such a crazy thing?"

"I'm the president of the video club at Hiawassee Middle," I supply. Adults always cut you more slack if they think something is a project for school.

It does the trick—especially when I promise to put an ad for The Shiny Bumper on the club's yearbook page. Sure, I get yelled at, but at least no one is talking about calling the cops anymore. The manager even sends one of his employees into the mechanism to rescue my glasses, which are undamaged except for a small crack in the right lens.

We head back to my place. I'm riding the trike, mostly because I'm too weak to stand. Chase carries the precious cargo—the two cameras with the footage on them.

"Sorry, Chase," I mumble, contrite. "I didn't mean to get you in trouble."

He cocks an eyebrow. "Looks more like you got me *out* of trouble."

"All I did was tell the truth. The whole thing was my idea."

"That guy was ready to have me arrested," he insists.

"Well," I tell him, "that's mostly because of your reputation—" Oops. "That is, your old reputation—you know, for stuff you probably don't even remember doing." In my depleted state, I'm not thinking straight. I'm digging my grave with my mouth.

He shakes his head. "*My* reputation wasn't what made the difference. That was all yours. You must be somebody pretty special around here to get that kind of reaction from a guy who runs a car wash."

I'm blown away. My record as a nerd and goody-two-shoes never seemed like much to me before. For sure, it didn't compare to Chase's—athlete, bad boy, big man on campus. But it was my reputation, not his, that got us out of a jam back there.

At my house, we manage to sneak upstairs without Mom getting a look at her baby boy in such a state of disrepair. I'd never be able to convince her that Chase didn't do it to me—a bully-palooza where I was half drowned in the river and had my glasses smashed by a ball-peen hammer.

I can barely bring myself to take the time to change out of my wet clothes. That's how anxious I am to see the footage we shot. I keep expecting Chase to lose interest and take off, but he hangs around, and it starts to sink in that he's just as into it as I am.

We watch the video from the GoPro first. It's pretty insane—a blizzard of flying foam and torrents of water, and a lot of whimpering I wasn't aware of at the time. I might have been trying to yell for help, but I couldn't form actual words. I was also thrashing around more than I remember. It's a miracle I stayed on the trike. The best part is when the brushes come. It's as if I'm being attacked by two whirling monsters from *Where the Wild Things Are*.

Next we play Chase's footage from the viewing area next to the washing tunnel. There I am, clinging to the tricycle like it's the only thing keeping me from floating away into outer space. When the freezing-cold water hits, my entire body writhes, belly dancer style, only at triple speed. And when the powerful dryer's on, you can actually see my skin pushed up against the bone structure of my skull. It's pure gold, and I have to say that a lot of the credit for that goes to Chase. He's got a real knack for camera work.

We laugh until we're falling over each other. It's definitely more fun to watch it than it was to go through it in real life. I show Chase how to piece the video together on the computer, intercutting footage from both cameras for maximum effect. For example, when you see the GoPro image flying all over the place, and then jump to me, jerking and flailing, struggling to keep my perch on the trike, it's even more hilarious because it explains why the picture inside the car wash is so wild and chaotic. Chase catches on quickly, and adds some good suggestions of his own, like a split screen of both cameras when the spin brushes come in.

At last, we set the whole thing to music—"Ride of the Valkyries"—and upload the clip to YouTube. We give it a title—*How to Clean Your Tricycle*, Brendan Espinoza and Chase Ambrose, coproducers. I kid you not, he actually thanks me when I include him in the credits.

We watch it on every device in the house—the computer, our phones, and an iPad. We even Chromecast it to the TV. It doesn't get old. If this video won't go viral, there's no justice in the world—or at least on YouTube.

He's still laughing as I see him out. "That might be the most fun I ever had!" I swear, he's like a kindergartner who's just been handed the world's most intricate balloon animal.

Without thinking, I reply, "How do you know? You've probably forgotten most of the fun you've had."

He looks surprised for a few seconds, and I figure I'm about to get his book bag in the side of the head. Then he says, "Good point. But it was still awesome."

Me and my big mouth, I can't leave well enough alone. "You know, we've got a video club at school, and you'd be a natural with your camera skills. We could really use you."

That might be the dumbest thing I've ever said aloud. Chase Ambrose and his football buddies have made a career out of terrorizing kids just like the vidiots. Recruiting him is like inviting a shark over for sushi.

He grins at me. "When's the next meeting?"

CHAPTER SEVEN

SHOSHANNA WEBER

He did it! The crazy fool actually did it!

We're gathered around the Smart Board in Ms. DeLeo's room, watching *How to Clean Your Tricycle* on YouTube. I've got to hand it to Brendan—when he sets his mind on something, he follows through, even after the entire video club told him to take a hike. And you know what? He knocked it out of the park. I've never seen anything so funny. It's a wonder he didn't get himself killed. But he's very much alive, beaming like a proud papa, as he premieres his work to rave reviews from the club.

Ms. DeLeo, our faculty advisor, laughs until tears are streaming down her cheeks. "Brendan, how could you even dream of doing such a thing?"

"The worst part was how cold the water was," he says. "But it was totally worth it."

We burst into thunderous applause when the music comes to a crescendo and the tricycle is pedaled out of The Shiny Bumper into the light. Brendan takes a bow, a goofy grin plastered onto his face.

Credits appear on the screen: PRODUCED BY BRENDAN ESPINOZA AND CHASE AMBROSE.

Chase Ambrose?

The ovation dies abruptly in the classroom.

"That's part of the joke, right?" Mauricia Dunbar offers dubiously. "Like produced by William Shakespeare or Mickey Mouse?"

"No, it was really him," Brendan tells us. "None of you guys would help me, and he said okay."

"Why would you even ask him?" I blurt, furious. "Do you have a death wish or something?"

Ms. DeLeo steps in. "Isn't it enough that the video got made and it's fabulous?"

"I don't have a death wish," Brendan retorts. "And you know what? I'm glad I asked him, because he did an awesome job on camera two. Maybe it's from sports, but he has a really steady hand. Better than any of us—including me. We could use a guy like that."

I get a sinking feeling in my gut. "You *didn't*!"

Brendan nods. "I invited him to join the club."

We all start babbling at the same time. I'm so angry that I can't really make out much of it. But it's pretty obvious that everybody is relating the story of some mean thing that Chase and probably Aaron and Bear did to them. There's definitely no shortage of material. The chorus of complaint goes on and on.

"Yeah, I get it!" Brendan holds up his hands. "Those guys picked on me too—more than any of you!"

Not more than my poor brother, I think.

"But the Chase Ambrose who worked on this video," Brendan goes on, "is not the same person. He lost his memory when he fell off his roof this summer—total amnesia. I know it sounds weird, but maybe he forgot what a jerk he was."

"Big talk from the guy who thinks riding a tricycle through a car wash is a smart thing to do," puts in Hugo.

Brendan doesn't back down. "Seriously—we had a great time yesterday. He was helpful. He had good ideas. He was even nice. He's *different*."

All I can see is a red haze in front of my eyes—and through it, Joel, packing his suitcase to go away to school.

I remind Brendan, "My brother would be in this room right now if it wasn't for that jerk! I don't want him here. None of us do."

"That's enough," Ms. DeLeo cuts me off. "School clubs are open to everyone. We don't pick and choose. If this boy wants to be a member, then we take him in. It's as simple as that."

The atmosphere in the room is supercharged—rage from me, defiance from Brendan, firmness from the teacher, and varying degrees of protest, discontent, and unease from everyone else. It boils around us when a voice from the doorway asks, "Am I late? What did I miss?"

It's him—the enemy.

He enters the room, tentative but smiling. And here I am unarmed, without my trusty tub of frozen yogurt.

"Welcome," Ms. DeLeo greets him. "Brendan was just showing us your new video. We're so happy you decided to join us."

Chase seems hesitant. He probably picks up on the disconnect between Ms. DeLeo's warm welcome and the body language coming off the rest of us. Only the KEEP OUT sign is missing. When he sees me, he takes a step back, a little fearful. The fear looks good on him. At least *that* part of his memory works. He remembers that I'm the person who hates his guts.

"*How to Clean Your Tricycle* killed," Brendan assures him. "And look—we already have forty-six views on YouTube. I was hoping it would be viral already, but these things take time."

"They call it viral because it's supposed to spread *fast*, like a virus," I put in sourly.

"Some viruses are slower than others," Brendan replies.

"So what exactly do you guys do?" Chase asks. "You know, when you're not riding tricycles through car washes?"

That bugs me too. For sure, that's how he sees us—a collection of nerdy wing nuts who pull off moronic stunts and call it brilliance. Brendan can be kind of a goofball, but he's also the smartest kid in school. A knuckle dragger like Chase will never appreciate someone who's destined to accomplish something that will make the world a better place. Why would he? The simplest way to make the world a better place would be to kick out Chase Ambrose.

Ms. DeLeo provides the answer. "Well, some of us will be working on entries for the National Video Journalism Contest."

"You mean just Shoshanna," Brendan snickers.

"If you could get your head out of YouTube long enough," I tell him, "you'd see what a great opportunity it is. This year's guideline is to profile a senior citizen with an interesting story to tell. We should all consider it."

"I don't think I know any old people," is Chase's reaction. Probably because he gets his jollies by pushing them out into traffic.

"We'll also be producing the school's video yearbook," the teacher goes on. "That's something you can sink your teeth into."

I cringe. Bad analogy for Chase, who I always pictured as a mountain lion picking over a carcass.

"What goes into a video yearbook?" Chase asks.

"Student interviews, mostly," Hugo jumps in. "You get so much more than the standard picture and quote." He shrinks back when he remembers who he's talking to. My brother's experience has trained us to avoid capturing Chase's attention. He can't target you if he doesn't notice you're there.

Chase nods. "Makes sense."

"Nifty way to keep score of the kids whose lives you've ruined over the year, isn't it?" I add bitterly.

He's thrown by that, but Ms. DeLeo jumps in quickly. "We'll also need content on every club and team in the school. Chase, since you play sports, I thought you'd be a natural to cover the athletic program."

A hopeful buzz greets this suggestion. Interviewing the jocks is a miserable job, since they're always so uncooperative and hostile. The worst of them is usually our newest member himself, but we've still got Aaron and Bear, plus Joey Petronus, Landon Rubio, and some of the others to contend with. It's like

Miss America. If the winner can't fulfill her duties, there are plenty of runners-up to take over the tiara.

"I'll try," says Chase. "But I don't really know those guys so well anymore. I mean, they know *me*—"

Well, how about that? Brendan's right—this big dummy fell on his ugly head hard enough to give himself amnesia. What other explanation could there be that he "doesn't really know" the juvenile co-delinquents that he's partnered with in a reign of terror that covers the entire town?

Could Brendan also be right that Chase has no idea what a jerk he is?

No. Amnesia can wipe out the details of your past, but it can't change the kind of person you are. Maybe he doesn't remember being a bully. He might have no clue that he tortured Joel to the point where he had no choice but to leave town. But when a person like that wants to know how he feels about something, and looks deep inside his black heart, it's still going to be filled with acid.

I message my theory to Joel later that night.

JWPianoMan: So what ur telling me is: I'm in exile, and the guy who exiled me doesn't even remember doing it?

Shosh466: That's what they say.

JWPianoMan: Don't know what 2 think about that.

Shosh466: He'll remember soon enough. Or Beta & Gamma Rats will remind him.

JWPianoMan: U seem 2 know a lot about Alpha Rat these days.

I start to tell Joel the real headline—who the video club's newest member is. My fingers freeze over my phone screen. My brother is depressed enough. The thought of Chase forcing him away and then parachuting into his spot in the club and ruining it will only make him feel worse.

No, that's not it. That slimeball didn't *ruin* video club. What really happened was even worse: nothing.

The worst person in the world came to Ms. DeLeo's room and . . . life went on. The other members didn't quit. The ceiling didn't cave in; our equipment didn't burst into flame. Ms. DeLeo didn't collapse at her desk.

We can't stand that guy, but we're going to put up with him. No way am I going to tell Joel that. He's upset enough as it is.

Besides, Chase Ambrose will last about ten minutes in video club. As soon as Ms. DeLeo actually asks him to *do* something, he'll be gone.

So I type:

Shosh466: Boring school, boring town. Amnesia = big news.

JWPianoMan: Alpha Rat squeezing zits = big news at that school.

Shosh466: He doesn't have any zits.

That's a pointless thing to text Joel. But by the time that occurs to me, I've already tapped send.

JWPianoMan: HMS kids r such morons.

Shosh466: Melton kids any better???

JWPianoMan: NO!!!

It's as if a deep chasm opens up in my stomach. I don't want to make him feel worse, but it needs to be said.

Shosh466: C'mon, little bro. U were miserable at home.

JWPianoMan: At least there I was special. Here I'm just another 2nd rate piano player.

I think of Chase and want to explode.

CHAPTER EIGHT

CHASE AMBROSE

The Hiawassee Middle School Hurricanes play a preseason scrimmage against East Norwich on Saturday. I make it a point to be there, not as a player, but as a member of the video club. Ms. DeLeo put me in charge of athletics for the video year-book, so the game is as good a place to start as any.

As I climb the bleachers, the flip-cam is an awkward weight in my hand. I don't feel like a video club kid—not that I can recall being *any* kind of kid. This is supposed to be the site of my greatest glories, yet I've lost all that. The sight of the players on the field doesn't bring back a rush of gridiron memories. I guess I always pictured vast crowds cheering my name, but there isn't much turnout for the scrimmage—maybe a couple of dozen kids and a handful of other people scattered around the stands.

I raise the camera and shoot a couple of plays. Brendan said I was a natural filming *How to Clean Your Tricycle.* That was easy, though. That stunt at the car wash was the craziest, fun-niest, most bizarre thing I've ever seen. I honestly couldn't look away. And since I was watching through the camera viewfinder, I captured the insanity from start to finish.

It would be wrong to say I had the time of my life, since I

can't speak for my life before the accident. But it was more than enough for Brendan to convince me that video club was the place for me.

A foghorn voice drowns out the PA announcement broadcasting over the loudspeaker. "Champ! Over here!"

It's my dad, sitting in the fourth row with Helene.

"I never miss a game," he exclaims, assuring me that he was here on the fifty-yard line, week in and week out, all through the twenty-eight-year gap between his state championship and my own. "Helene's turning into a real fan too."

My half sister has set up an impressive array of dollhouse furniture on the metal bleachers and is playing with a couple of Barbies. As far as I've seen, she hasn't looked in the direction of the field once.

For such a big Hurricanes fan, Dad sure doesn't seem to have any fun watching them play. The longer we sit, the darker his mood gets, blackening and lowering until it hangs over him like a line of thunderheads.

"Did you see that?" he complains. "The left guard is supposed to cut block on that play! Otherwise, there's no hole for the running back!" Or: "Our quarterback doesn't see the field! He had a man wide open in the end zone!" Or: "What kind of tackling is that? Did you used to tackle like that? I never tackled like that!"

"I don't remember anything about playing football," I tell him honestly, zooming in tight on the huddle. "So I have no idea how I used to tackle."

"Yeah, well, it was a lot better than that," he snorts. "You used to wrap up your man and bring him down properly." By this time, the Hurricanes are on the wrong end of a 24–7 score.

It's funny—I've forgotten everything about my own football career, but I know the game itself. When I shoot footage of the action on the field, I get what the players are doing—or at least trying to do. Either East Norwich is all-universe, or this year's Hiawassee Hurricanes aren't a team of destiny. I have no idea how good I am, but it's hard to believe that one person could make up the difference between these stumblebums and last year's state champions.

"We're out of sync," I observe. "The O-line is opening up some good holes, but the backs are never in the right place to run through them."

"Exactly!" Dad slaps me too hard on my bad shoulder. "That's what *I* always say! We've got the talent—we do when you're on the field, anyway. All we need is the *timing*!"

I'm sure it isn't the first time my father and I have ever agreed on something, but it's the first time I actually remember. That's another thing amnesia made me forget—how much I like his approval.

Helene has dismantled her Barbie condo on the bleachers and is bored out of her mind. "Daddy, can we *leave*?"

"Not yet, honey." Dad doesn't even glance away from the field. "It's still the third quarter."

I point the flip-cam at her. "Why don't you set up the furniture again? We can make a movie about your dolls."

She curls her lip at me. "They're *Barbies*."

"Barbie can be a movie star," I offer.

As she places the plastic chairs and tables with great care, quarterback Joey Petronus throws an interception that East Norwich runs back for yet another touchdown.

That does it for Dad. He goes off on a diatribe against the players, the coaches, even the guys who make the chalk lines on the field. I'm not immune either. He finishes with, "What are you doing with that camera, anyway? You should be *in* this game, not taking pictures of it! I know you don't remember how good you are—but, I promise you, you are *that good*."

I start to tell him I'm only here to cover the team for the video yearbook, but something makes me swallow the words before they hit air. I understand on a gut level that isn't what Dad wants to hear.

Instead, I find myself saying, "I want to get back on the field. As soon as the doctor gives the okay. You'll see. I'll be out there."

Dad nods, pleased. "That's who we are, Champ. We're Ambrose men. We're the doers. Other people take pictures of *us*!"

Helene acts out entire story lines with her Barbies. I capture it on video, all the while keeping up a running game commentary with Dad, who doesn't seem to be a Barbie guy, surprise, surprise.

When I play my footage back to Helene on the tiny screen, she squeals with delight.

And there, sitting on the bleachers in front of a bad football game, it happens.

I *remember*.

I mean, there's nothing wrong with my *ability* to remember. I remember everything that's happened *since* I woke up in the hospital. But before the accident—except for that weird image of the girl in blue—nothing.

Until now.

It's a flashback of Helene. She's probably what triggered it, because in my memory, she's squealing just like she is now.

Wait—no. It isn't a happy sound. Her cheeks are red, her face twisted, and she's about to bawl.

In the memory, I'm holding a stuffed teddy—her *favorite.* I remember that too. Actually, I've got the bear in my left hand—and its head in my right.

I ripped the head off a four-year-old's teddy bear!

Definitely not the memory I'd been hoping for. But still . . .

"I remembered something!" I exclaim out loud.

"Yeah, what?" Dad actually turns his attention from the game.

"Something from before the accident!"

"See?" He's triumphant. "I told you there's nothing wrong with you. You'll be back in commission in no time. And, man, do we ever need you out there!"

On the field, our halfback takes a handoff and is buried under a pile of East Norwich jerseys. Dad's looking away, so he misses it—a tiny gap in the weak side of the defensive line.

Our guy could have hit that. *I* would have hit that!

A stutter-step to the left—that's what I would have done. Juke out the linebacker, and . . . *gone*! My shoulders shimmy as I make the imaginary cuts in my head.

I see it now. I was a *player*!

Correction: I *am* a player. And as I picture it, the image of the headless teddy bear starts to fade.

After all, it's just a stuffed toy. Helene is perfectly happy now. No harm, no foul.

I'll bet she's forgotten it ever happened.

CHAPTER NINE

CHASE AMBROSE

After the scrimmage, I head down to the locker room to get some player interviews. I arrive just in time to see Aaron slamming the heavy metal door in Hugo's face. He staggers backward straight into me, and lets out a whoop of shock.

"Take it easy, Hugo," I tell him. "It's just me."

"Hi, Chase," he manages, his voice faltering. "I'm trying to shoot some footage of the team." He hefts his own flip-cam.

"I thought Ms. DeLeo put me on that," I tell him.

"Oh, sure, totally," he says quickly. "We were just afraid you might, you know, forget."

"What do you mean, forget?" I ask, a little annoyed.

He retreats a step, blushing and looking plenty worried. "N-n-no offense," he stammers.

Before I can reply, the door opens and there's Bear.

"I told you it was his voice!" he shouts. He hauls me inside, shutting Hugo out again.

"Hugo's with me," I protest.

"Ha—good one!" Bear laughs.

"Seriously. We're covering the Hurricanes for the video yearbook."

So Hugo gets in with me. He's grateful, but it doesn't make him very happy. He acts like he's tiptoeing around a minefield.

I get some high fives, but the team's not in the best spirits. After all, they just got steamrolled. And when it sinks in that I'm there as a reporter, and not to give them the good news that I've been cleared to play, they can't hide their disappointment.

"Well, I can't see anything wrong with you," Joey complains. "You're not even in that sling anymore."

I get it. Joey laid an egg at quarterback today. A good running game would take a lot of pressure off him.

"It's the concussion," I try to explain. "The doctor wants me to be really careful."

Landon Rubio—the kid with the giant neck I saw on the first day—glances dubiously from Hugo to me. "So you have to miss a few games. But what gives with *him*?"

Hugo attempts to point his camera and is beaten back by a hail of dirty sweat socks.

I bristle. "The video yearbook is doing a segment on every sports team including golf and badminton. So when you're not in it, don't come crying to us."

"Yearbook?" Joey echoes. "Bad enough you're off the team. Now you're on yearbook staff?"

"*Video* yearbook," Hugo amends.

A snapping towel nearly takes his ear off.

"Guys—chill out!" Aaron steps between the other players and Hugo and me. "It isn't our boy's fault his doctor's a wuss! Cut him some slack!"

"That doesn't explain why he's running around with the video losers," Landon challenges.

"He's not running around with anybody," Aaron explains reasonably. "He's covering the Hurricanes, man, making sure we look good in that yearbook thing. That's how he's helping the team while he's on the sidelines."

"Yeah, Rubio," snorts Bear. "If I had a face like yours, I'd appreciate anyone who could make me look good. So shut up."

I jump in as peacemaker. "Believe me, guys—I'll be back as soon as I get the word from my doctor."

This makes the team happy, I can tell. Hugo shoots me a strange look, but how can I expect him to understand? He doesn't strike me as the kind of guy who plays sports—except maybe in video games.

Joey chucks a ball my way. I watch, almost as a spectator, as my hands reach out and snatch it from the air. *Reaction time: A-OK.*

It feels good—like I'm back to an old self amnesia couldn't quite rob me of.

We do a few interviews. The guys are chatty with me, hamming it up for the camera like I'm running a selfie service. Hugo gets mostly one-word answers. When I notice, he mumbles that we can fix it in editing. I don't see how any amount of editing can fix: *Q: What are your thoughts for the upcoming season? A: Good.*

Then again, I'm just the newbie nobody even trusts to show up for my first video club assignment.

When we're done, Hugo can't get out of there fast enough. This is hostile territory for him. But me? I feel like I'm home.

"Well, I'd love to talk your ear off about my road to NFL glory," Aaron drawls, "but Bear and I have to go water some old people."

"Wait—I'm going with you," I tell them.

They stare at me like I've just announced that I'm flying to Jupiter.

"Dude, you don't have to go," Aaron reminds me. "They cut you loose because you got hurt."

"It'll be—fun." That falls flat, so I try again. "We're teammates, right? You go, I go."

Bear's eyes narrow. "Exactly how much do you remember about the Graybeard Motel?"

"Nothing," I reply honestly.

He grins. "If you want to go there when you don't have to, you didn't just scramble your brains. You knocked them out completely!"

"Come on, how bad can it be?" I'm semi-joking, but those two are so stone-faced that I start to wonder, *Yikes, what is this place—Frankenstein's lab?*

"Your call," Aaron says. "It'll be good to have you back with us—even if you're nuts."

The Portland Street Assisted Living Residence is about a ten-minute walk from school. I know I was on community service here before, but the place is brand-new to me. It's a boring three-story building with a wide circular drive and a broad landscaped front dotted with benches and outdoor picnic tables. There are several elderly people outside, enjoying the warm weather. A couple of them wave and call out greetings to us. I wave back. Aaron and Bear ignore them.

As the main door slides open in front of us, Bear mumbles, "Hold your breath."

It's an odd combination of two smells that don't mix—fresh flowers and hospital-like antiseptic. Not great, but you get used to it in a hurry.

We report to Nurse Duncan, who's the head nurse on duty. She's surprised to see me.

"I got better," I tell her. "So I figured I should finish off my community service."

"The court told you that?" she asks dubiously.

I shake my head. "I came up with it on my own."

"We don't believe it either," Aaron jokes with mock solemnity.

"That's very—noble," Nurse Duncan says. "Well, I've got you boys on the snack cart today. It doesn't normally take three, but we'll give Chase a soft job on his first day back."

We get a rolling cart laden with juice boxes, cookies, crackers, and free newspapers. By the time we get off the elevator on the third floor, Aaron and Bear have helped themselves to half the merchandise.

"Believe me, they have more Oreos than these mummies could ever gum down," Aaron says when I look disapproving. "And, I assure you, oh perfect one—you've sampled plenty of cookies off this cart."

I reach back for a snack-jacking memory, but come up empty. I'll have to take his word for it.

Bear tears open a bag and dumps a small pile of ginger-snaps into my hand. I take a tiny bite, glaring at my partners in crime, who are chowing down in a blizzard of wrappers and crumbs.

"We played a football game this morning," Bear reminds me. "You work up an appetite. Not everybody's too delicate, like you."

"I guess I'm not too delicate to bend over and pick up your garbage," I snap back. I might be getting the hang of being friends with these two.

We go door-to-door, offering the residents snacks and papers. When I was in the hospital, all the staff and volunteers who came into my room were really nice and friendly. Well, Aaron and Bear are the opposite of that. Aaron's the polite one. He flings the door wide and barks, "Snack cart!" This is followed by a "What do you want?" from Bear.

They call all the men Dumbledore and all the women Dumbledora and respond to any questions with a combination of shrugs and grunts. When I can't stand it anymore, I ask what I can do for everybody, and usually end up adjusting bed heights, searching for lost TV remotes, and occasionally calling nurses.

"You're slowing us down, man," Aaron complains. "At this rate, we'll never blow this Geritol stand."

"Quiet!" I hiss. "They'll hear you!"

"You're joking, right?" Bear sneers. "Most of these old

fossils can't remember to change the batteries in their hearing aids. The last thing any of them heard was the A-bomb test at Yucca Flat."

"They're not as deaf as you think," I shoot back. "The lady in two-twelve definitely heard it when you ripped one in her living room."

Aaron laughs. "Now *that's* the Chase we know and love."

Those jokes are funny when it's the three of us; not so much when the old people are around. Most of them are pretty frail. They definitely deserve more respect than they're getting from us. Maybe Aaron and Bear ran out of patience because they've got no choice about community service and I'm here on purpose. Maybe I was out of patience too before my amnesia made me forget it. But I find the residents kind of interesting. They remember stuff in real life that you can only read about in history books. There's a lady in 326 whose father was one of the firemen on the scene of the *Hindenburg* disaster. The guy in 318 was a communications expert at Houston Mission Control when Neil Armstrong first set foot on the moon. In room 209 lives a guy who's totally blind, yet tells the most vivid stories of growing up two doors down from Baseball Hall of Famer Joe DiMaggio.

The rule is that if someone is not in or sleeping, we leave a juice box and a packet of cookies on the table. The man in 121 is snoring enthusiastically in an easy chair when I notice the black-and-white photo on his nightstand. It's a picture of a young soldier bowing his head to receive a military decoration from an important-looking man with round steel-rimmed spectacles.

"Is that President Truman?" I whisper.

Aaron looks bored. "Who cares? Let's get out of here. If this Dumbledore wakes up, he'll talk your ear off."

But I'm hooked. "The only medal you get straight from the president is the Medal of Honor. This guy's a hero."

"Big deal," Bear scoffs. "Back in the day there were so many wars that they handed out medals like Hershey's Kisses."

I sigh and start to follow them to the door. "I wonder what he did. They don't give out the Medal of Honor for just any old thing."

"Probably slew a triceratops or something," Aaron suggests with a shrug. "Come on. We're almost done."

"It was a pterodactyl," comes a sarcastic voice from behind us.

We wheel around. He's sitting up now, an elderly man, a little bent at the shoulders, with a shock of white hair.

"And I slew it with my stone knife."

I step forward. "Mister, that's you in the picture, right?"

"No, it's Harry Truman. Can't you see I'm busy? It takes me half an hour to get out of bed and twice that to haul myself across the room with this stupid walker."

He's obviously not busy. He just wants to be left alone. Maybe he doesn't like us very much. Apparently, not all the residents are hard of hearing.

Aaron and Bear are already slouching out of the room. "Sorry," I mumble, following them into the hall.

"You've got a lot to learn, Ambrose," Aaron tells me. "Get one of these Dumbledores talking about his war days and you'll be here till you're as old as he is."

I have to admit, it's probably good advice. "All right," I say. "Let's just finish."

We work our way down the hall to the last room on the floor. "Almost done," Aaron groans. "Just Cloud Ten and we can get out of here."

"Cloud Ten?" I echo.

"You're going to love this one," Bear assures me. "You know Cloud Nine? Well, this old bag's at least one cloud up from that. Half the time she's convinced this is some fancy hotel and we're room service."

I see their point, but I feel kind of bad for Mrs. Swanson, who bustles around her living room in a frilly pink dressing gown dotted with sequined flowers. She's obviously losing touch with reality, and there's nothing hilarious about that. At first she thinks we've come for a visit, and she asks us to move the furniture into what she calls a "conversation grouping."

Aaron and Bear ignore her, but what harm will it do, really? So I shuffle a few chairs, no big deal. My friends are mugging at me behind her back the whole time, trying to make me laugh. They might be the smart ones. By the time I'm finished, sweaty and breathing hard, Mrs. Swanson is looking at me like she's too polite to ask who I am and why I'm rearranging her apartment. Aaron and Bear are snickering out loud now.

We drop off her cookies and juice and head for the door, but she comes bustling after us, waving her pocketbook. She digs around, comes up with a twenty-dollar bill, and offers it to me.

"Don't leave without your tip," she says.

I take a step back. "Oh, no, I couldn't accept—"

Before I can manage another word, Bear's meaty hand snatches the money away. "Enjoy your stay," he tells Mrs. Swanson with a big phony smile. And he's out the door like a shot, Aaron hot on his heels.

I catch up to them in the hall. "You can't take that money! That's like stealing!"

"No, it's not," Bear replies. "She gave it to me. Actually, she gave it to *you*, but you were too dumb to take it."

"Yeah, but"—I fumble for the right words—"you know as well as I do that the lady's not all there."

"That's discrimination," he says righteously. "I'm not biased against dizzy old bats who haven't got a clue what the deal is. They can give me money just like everybody else. You don't know her—she would have gotten really upset if we hadn't taken it. She wants to believe what she believes."

"We're not here for kicks, you know," I insist. "We got sent here by a judge. If we get caught accepting money from the residents, we could get a lot more than community service."

Bear rounds on me in genuine amazement. "You don't even have to be here, man! You made us bring you!"

I'm stubborn. "Give the money back."

Aaron tries to be reasonable. "The museum pieces in this dump—they'd forget their own saggy butts if they weren't attached. By the time the door closed behind us, I guarantee Cloud Ten forgot we were ever there. If we go to her and try to straighten this out, it'll be like showing her how crazy she is. You want to be responsible for that?"

I know he's snowing me, but he's also kind of right. I doubt we could explain to Mrs. Swanson that she just tipped the community service guys. But even if we could, she'd be embarrassed and upset and probably more confused than before.

"We should give that money to charity," I mumble.

"Done," Bear agrees. "It's going to my favorite charity—the Take a Bear to Lunch Fund. Who's up for pizza?"

We all laugh—but I'm laughing a lot less than those two. The whole thing leaves a sour taste in my mouth, and pizza is the last thing I'm thinking about.

We stop in to see Nurse Duncan so Aaron and Bear can get their time sheets signed. I'm not technically on community service anymore, so there's no time sheet for me.

Then we're heading for the pizza place like nothing ever happened. I keep looking at Bear, expecting to see the twenty glowing orange and burning through the pocket of his jeans. I can't explain it, but the more they goof around, tripping and shoving each other, the less appetite I have for lunch.

"You okay, Ambrose?" Aaron tosses at me in concern. "You don't look so hot."

"I—I'll catch up with you guys later!"

I pound back in the direction of Portland Street. I hang a left and sprint up to the assisted living residence, then dash in the sliding door and straight to room 100.

I pull a fistful of crumpled bills from my pocket and fish out a twenty. Aaron's right—I'd never be able to explain to Mrs. Swanson why I'm giving her money for what she could only see as no reason. No, my plan is simpler than that: I'll slip it right under her door. When she notices it, she'll just assume she dropped it.

As I squat down and pass the bill through the gap between the door and the carpet, it occurs to me that if anybody sees me, it'll look like I'm the one doing something sleazy, not the one making it right. Luck is with me, though. I'm able to return the twenty unobserved.

No, not "return," I remind myself. I'm out twenty bucks in this deal. I feel a little resentful when I picture Aaron and Bear feasting on pizza that I'm essentially paying for. But it's a small price tag for being able to sleep at night.

As I make my way out again, I pause in front of 121—the Medal of Honor guy's room. I squint at the small plaque on the wall: MR. JULIUS SOLWAY.

The door is open a crack, and I catch a glimpse of Mr. Solway struggling across the room on his walker. Suddenly, a baleful eye is glaring at me through the opening.

"You're back?" Mr. Solway's raspy voice growls from inside. "What do you want now?"

My instinct is to flee, but curiosity gets the better of me.

"Which war was it?" I ask the old man. "You know, where you won the medal?"

"The Trojan War," he barks. "Remember Achilles? I was the one who got him right in the heel."

It stings, but I say, "I didn't mean to disturb you," and start away.

"Korea," he calls after my retreating back. "1952."

I turn. "It's an honor to meet you, Mr. Solway. You must have done something really heroic."

"Everyone did," he replies gruffly. "A lot of brave men are still buried there. They're the heroes. I'm just the one they picked to hang a bauble on."

I can't help asking. "What did you do? To earn the medal, I mean."

I can still only see one eye, but it's impossible to miss the flash of impatience. "I stood on my head and spit nickels. Listen, smart guy, when you get to be my age, you don't always remember the details of every single event in your life. But I don't expect a young punk like you to understand that." He closes the door.

Old people are supposed to have wisdom, but Mr. Solway is definitely wrong about me.

I've already forgotten more than he'll ever know.

CHAPTER TEN

KIMBERLY TOOLEY

I love pep rallies.

I love the noise and the cheering. I love being with the whole school, packed onto the bleachers in the gym, showing our spirit and raising the roof, stomping and screaming our heads off. (Getting out of class doesn't hurt either.)

I'm a huge football fan. It's definitely my favorite sport. All those downs are kind of confusing, though—first down, second down, touchdown, down by contact, illegal man downfield. Hard to figure out. But when the Hiawassee Hurricanes thunder onto the field with their shoulder pads, it's all good. Guys look amazing in shoulder pads.

This season might not be as awesome as usual because Chase Ambrose isn't on the team. Chase is our star, and out of all the players who look good in shoulder pads, he looks the best. He hurt himself falling off a roof this summer, and the word around school is that he has amnesia. He can't remember anything—including the fact that I've had a crush on him since sixth grade, and he doesn't even know I'm alive.

So he isn't one of the players in full uniform showing off on the gym floor while we stomp and cheer. Oh, he's down there, all right—recording the goings-on with a video camera. I don't really get that part. It's one thing for Chase to be off the team. It's quite another for him to join the video club. (Those kids are basically nerds.)

The point of the rally is to get everyone all riled up to annihilate Jefferson on Saturday. So we've got dummies dressed in Jefferson jerseys, and our guys are kicking the stuffing out of them. And our mascot is beating up Jefferson's mascot (actually just a Hiawassee kid in a jaguar suit). Chase is filming them close-up, holding his camera right in there to capture every fake punch. I miss the shoulder pads, but he still looks good.

And then the rally's over. We file off the bleachers and start for our lockers to get our stuff to go home. The team heads out to practice, clattering down the hallway that leads to the field house. There's a bit of a traffic jam there—players going one way and the rest of us going the other. A few elbows fly.

Brendan Espinoza somehow gets bumped into the path of the players. (That's typical Brendan, who could cross an empty parking lot and slip on the one banana peel in the middle.) The guys know Brendan, and make a game of bouncing him around like he's a soccer ball. Pretty soon, the team is laughing, the kids are laughing, and Brendan is flying back and forth, holding on to his camera for dear life. It's pretty funny.

A chant goes up while Brendan flails. It's like the whole football team is calling out, "Pass it! . . . Pass it! . . . Pass it!"

There's a blur of motion, and suddenly Joey Petronus is slammed up against the wall by two fistfuls of his football jersey. It's Chase! His handsome face is normally chiller than chill. But right now, it's boiling mad.

"Let the kid go!" Chase demands.

Brendan stumbles free, collapsing to the opposite wall.

The other Hurricanes haul Chase off Joey, and there's a lot of shoving going on. Shoving comes naturally to football players. (It's even part of the game. Every play starts off with two lines of guys shoving each other.)

Two Hurricanes hold Chase, struggling, by the arms. Chase looks almost small, dwarfed by all those players in pads and cleats.

Aaron and Bear muscle into the center of the action, putting themselves between Joey and Chase.

"Dial it down!" Aaron orders. "We're all teammates here."

"What did that guy ever do to you, huh?" Chase spits at Joey, yanking his arms free.

"Like you've got anything to say about it!" Joey shoots back.

"What's that supposed to mean?"

Joey indicates Brendan, who's dusting himself off, surrounded by his fellow video clubbers. "Yeah, right. Like you never had a little fun with Espinoza."

I laugh at that one, because no one messed with the dweebs more than Chase, Aaron, and Bear. But Chase looks so mystified that it hits me: If he really has amnesia, is it possible that he doesn't remember?

Chase addresses the entire team. "We were shooting *your* pep rally to make *you* look good. You're welcome."

The players stare at him in horror. He has no clue what he said to upset them, but I do.

He said *we*.

(*We*, the video club. *You*, the team.)

Joey hefts his helmet. "We used to be tight with this kid Chase Ambrose. We were more than teammates; we were *boys*. But lately, I don't even know who he is." He leads the Hurricanes in a jog out to the field.

Aaron and Bear hang back. I'm expecting them to take Chase's side, since those three are best friends. Chase seems pretty shocked when Bear wheels off with the others.

Aaron eyes Chase with a long face. "You shouldn't have done that, man. Joey's your friend. He's had your back plenty of times."

Chase is still defiant, but a little more subdued than before. "So I should just let him beat up a kid half his size for no reason?"

Aaron stands his ground. "If you'd told him to stop, he would have stopped. You didn't have to *attack* him." He shakes his head. "None of us are perfect—not even you. Next time, take a second to think about who your friends are."

He disappears after the team.

"Thanks, Chase," Brendan says in a shaky voice.

Shy but grateful, the video club members express their gratitude. Not too many people ever stand up to the football team. Only Chase can do it, because he's one of them.

At least he used to be.

Shoshanna Weber rolls her eyes. "Please be real! Why would anybody thank *him*? Is there any one of us he hasn't treated like garbage?"

Brendan looks at her in surprise. "Didn't you see what happened there?"

"I saw him being a *goon*, like he always is. Today he was on our side. What about tomorrow? Remember what he did to my brother!" She storms off.

Wow, Joel Weber. Just thinking about him puts a lump in my throat. I almost forgot he's Shoshanna's brother. A lot of this stuff feels kind of harmless until something like Joel Weber happens.

Chase seems a little shell-shocked by the whole thing. After all, he took on the football team on behalf of the video club kids. And what's his reward? Getting dissed by one of them.

The others try to smooth it over.

"Sorry, man."

"She didn't mean it."

"You were awesome back there."

Brendan is last. "You didn't have to do that," he says. (Although it's pretty obvious he's glad someone came to his rescue.)

Then they're gone. The hallway has cleared out by now, so it's just Chase and me.

He's still bewildered. "I didn't even know she had a brother."

"Yeah, Joel Weber. Quiet kid, plays piano. He got bullied so bad that his folks sent him away to boarding school."

That's the edited version of the truth. What Chase doesn't remember is he basically starred in that bullying. I don't think his goal could have been to force Joel to leave town, but he definitely intended to make him miserable. I wonder if he was sorry when he heard that the Webers were sending their son away.

I guess no one will ever know, not even Chase himself. However he felt about what happened to Joel, he's already forgotten it.

Chase chews it over. "I was in on that, wasn't I?" he says finally. "I was in on a lot of stuff. People look at me funny around here, and maybe it's not just because I'm the idiot who fell off a roof."

"No one thinks you're an idiot," I put in quickly.

"Yeah, but it isn't the kind of thing Albert Einstein ever did." He pauses thoughtfully (a good look for him—makes him seem older). "You can't believe how weird it is to have this whole life, and everyone remembers it except you."

"I'm Kimberly," I tell him. "But you always call me Kimmy." Not exactly true, but how's he ever going to know? I always wanted to be called Kimmy, especially by him.

We shake hands like two businesspeople meeting for the first time.

"Well, I'm late for video club," he tells me. "See you—Kimmy."

I'm speechless, so I just wave at him.

This has to be the best day ever. If Chase forgot everything, it means he also doesn't remember that he's totally out of my league.

I have to join the video club as soon as possible.

CHAPTER ELEVEN

AARON HAKIMIAN

My dad always uses this expression: "If it looks like a duck, and it quacks like a duck, it's probably a duck."

Well, that isn't always true. It looks like Ambrose, and it talks like Ambrose. But no way that's Ambrose.

How can a person be so different just because he fell on his head? Okay, so he's sidelined from football. Nothing you can do about some dumb doctor's orders. And amnesia. That's pretty out there, although Wikipedia says it's real.

But even if every single memory is erased from your head—wiped clean like my phone when I dropped it in the toilet—you should still be the same person, right?

Chase just isn't. That's not the kid Bear and I grew up with, played sports with, broke all the rules with, since we were in second grade.

You can see it in his eyes. He looks at us like he barely knows us—or any of the Hurricanes. I guess I understand that. We're like new people he just met for the first time. Even so, shouldn't we be starting to hit it off by now? That's not happening either. He's not into the things we're into. Not football, not anything.

That hurts. I get that his memory is erased. But is our whole friendship erased too? Being boys with someone isn't just a bunch of stuff you did together in the past. There has to be more to it than that! But right now, it's like we've got zero in common with the guy.

Worse, the kids he *does* have stuff in common with are all *losers*! The video club—really? The Chase I knew whaled on those guys worse than any of us! And now *they're* who he wants to hang out with? Who's next, huh? The Care Bears? And those wusses have totally forgiven him too—except Shoshanna, for obvious reasons. I wonder if he's figured *that* out yet.

The big question is this: Is the old Ambrose trapped in there somewhere waiting to realize what a dork he's being and get back to normal? Or is this new nerd-loving Chase the only Chase there's going to be from now on?

That's a pretty big deal, and not just because we're supposed to be boys. He has something that belongs to all three of us—something *important*. What if he doesn't even know he's got it?

Bear isn't a deep thinker. He's all action. "Dude, this is stupid. Let's just ask him. Say, 'We know you have it; fork it over.'"

"The guy has amnesia," I reason. "That means he might not even remember where he put it."

Bear snorts. "You buy that? Trust me, he remembers just fine. That thing's valuable. He's faking all this amnesia stuff so he can keep it for himself."

"You're talking about our boy!" I exclaim angrily, giving him a shove that would put one of those video dweebs halfway across town. "You're a jerk for even thinking it!"

He shoves me back. "Then you're the jerk, because I know you're thinking it too."

But I'm not thinking it. Honestly, if Chase is just punking us all with this amnesia stuff, that would be better. If tomorrow he says, "Fooled you!" I might be ticked off for a day or so. Then I'd shake his hand for putting one over on us.

Mostly, I'd be glad to have the old Chase back.

"One way or the other, we've got a problem," I tell him. "If we face him with it, and he honestly doesn't remember, then we've just confessed to a guy who isn't really our friend anymore."

"Big deal."

"It *is* a big deal," I persist. "Because the new Chase is a goody-goody. He stands up for losers; he does community service when he doesn't have to. If he forgot what we did, I don't want to remind him. A guy like that could turn all three of us in because it's The Right Thing To Do."

"Unless he's lying," Bear adds grimly.

"And we'll deal with that too—if necessary. We'll just have to wait and see."

There's nothing more frustrating than trying to squeeze the truth out of someone when you can't let him know what you're trying to get him to say. I'm a plain guy. I like plain talk. But in this case, it's too dangerous.

Our best chance to coax it out of him is at the Graybeard Motel. But it's not so easy there either. Bad enough he does community service when he's off the hook; why does he have to be so gung ho about it? It's depressing to watch him. He delivers more snacks in twenty minutes than Bear and I could stretch into a whole afternoon. And in that extra time, he reads to people. He pushes wheelchairs around. He helps the old fogeys with cell phones they don't have a prayer of figuring out.

"Is it just me," Bear mutters, "or is he deliberately trying to make us look bad?"

"I don't think it's on purpose," I mumble back. "He really likes it here."

The old fossils like him too. We can't walk three feet down the hall without some Dumbledore or Dumbledora hauling him in to adjust the TV or to reach something from a high shelf.

Bear is insulted. "We're taller than Ambrose. We can reach stuff. How come nobody ever asks *us*?"

"Because we'd say no," I remind him. "Or maybe just ignore them. Listen, it's annoying that all these blue-hairs love Chase, but it's not a mystery."

Even sour-faced Nurse Duncan, who wishes our community service was over even more than we do, has a smile for Ambrose—and an even deeper scowl for Bear and me.

It doesn't help that Chase has forged the closest friendship of all with the one resident he should be staying away from—that crotchety old warhorse in room 121. Wouldn't you know it? The one graybeard who hates everybody—and who all the other graybeards hate right back—has decided to love Ambrose. Go figure.

It's those stupid Korean War stories that brought the two of them together. Chase can't get enough of them. And the geezer is overjoyed to have someone willing to listen who doesn't have to change his hearing-aid battery five times in the course of it.

"How come you guys have so much to say to each other?" Bear demands.

Ambrose shrugs. "He's interesting. It's not every day you meet somebody who's been awarded the country's highest medal."

Why does he always have to bring that up? It makes me nervous. And it makes Bear practically crazy.

"Wikipedia says the Korean War only lasted three years," I grumble. "He's already told you every minute of it. What more is there to say?"

Ambrose laughs. "He's nice."

"He's *not* nice. Ask anybody in the building. He calls noise complaints on squeaky wheelchairs. He yells out spoilers on movie night. The nurses hate him even worse than we do. If this was a reality show and they got to vote somebody out of the Graybeard Motel, he'd be on the street."

But Chase gets called away to wheel Mrs. Bergland to her weekly canasta game—as if one of the orderlies couldn't do it.

"Maybe he just likes war stories," I offer to Bear.

He isn't buying it. "He never liked war stories before."

And that's the whole problem. We know the kid—but we don't. Which makes it almost impossible to figure out what's going on inside his head.

Or how worried we should be.

CHAPTER TWELVE

CHASE AMBROSE

A few more memories have come back.

Mostly, it's just images and impressions, but there's one that's pretty concrete. My mother has been showing me a lot of old pictures in the hope that something might ring a bell. One snapshot of an ivy-covered building looks kind of familiar—the student union at Johnny's university, Mom explains.

It triggers a flashback. It's not that I *remember* it; more like it's already in my head, and I'm just noticing it now.

Mom and seventh-grade Chase are dropping Johnny off at college. Our car pulls around the long circular drive in front of the building in the photograph. Johnny gets out. It's his first day of freshman year, his first time living away from home. He seems terrified.

And what do I feel? Sympathy for my poor scared brother? Or for Mom, who's on the verge of tears? For myself, even—I'll be losing my brother to a new life in a faraway place.

I don't feel any of those things. Instead, I'm thinking: *What a wuss this kid is! I can't believe I ever looked up to him! What a wimp! What a baby!*

My scorn is so sharp that it jolts me back to the here and now. How could I have made such harsh judgments about my own brother? When I was in the hospital, Johnny was there at my bedside every minute Mom was, just as worried about me, just as torn up by my accident.

I guess that wasn't payback for the wonderful brotherly loyalty I've shown him over the years.

People say I've changed. I'm barely beginning to understand how much.

Dr. Cooperman isn't surprised that my memory is returning. My brain is totally fine, he says at my next appointment. After all, I remember everything that's happened *since* coming out of the coma. Not that it would be easy to forget things like Shoshanna dumping frozen yogurt on my head or Brendan going through the car wash on a tricycle. Or how it felt to push Joey against the wall—a blur of violence, anger, and lightning-fast action. And something else too—I may not be proud of it, but it's the truth: *satisfaction*. I didn't like the way a situation was going and I changed it with my own physical power.

Aaron's words come back to me: *You didn't have to attack him*. And Shoshanna's: *Goon*. That haunts me a little. I don't regret stopping Joey from bullying Brendan, but was fighting really the only way to make that happen? Worse, I didn't even *consider* trying to talk Joey down. I just grabbed the kid and manhandled him—the same way he was manhandling Brendan.

I get that the old Chase could be like that—before the accident. But now I'm starting to wonder if that person is still inside me, emerging from the darkness, bit by bit, along with my memory.

As weird as it was to lose my past, this might be even weirder: The more that comes back, the less I recognize myself.

Dr. Cooperman also pronounces me fully recovered physically. Then he drops the bomb: He still wants me off football for the rest of the season.

I must seem pretty devastated, because he adds, "It's all out of an abundance of caution. You're fine. But concussions can't be taken lightly. We're learning new things about the long-term effects every day."

"I know you're disappointed, honey," my mom adds. "I understand how important football is to you."

How can I explain it to them? Sure, I'd love to play, but what really bugs me is that football is my biggest connection to my old life. I don't think I've had a single conversation with Dad that wasn't about either my past gridiron glories or the ones he still expects me to have. And since the incident with Joey, the only Hurricanes who'll talk to me are Aaron and Bear. Even with them, half the time I get the impression that their main interest is getting their team captain back. For sure, those guys are never going to forgive me for a) doing my community service when I don't have to, and b) not hating it enough.

To be honest, I don't hate it at all. One thing no one ever tells you when you're laid up—like I was in the hospital—is how boring it is. You really appreciate anybody who comes to break the monotony. So now I get to be that person for the residents of Portland Street. It makes me feel good about myself.

And that's huge at a time when I'm learning I have so much to feel bad about.

Besides, I get stuff out of it too. I've learned how to play mah-jong, and I've picked up a lot of great tips on how to grow stuff, mostly from Mrs. Kittredge, whose room looks like a botanical garden. I think I'm going to be able to save a lot of Mom's plants, and maybe even the ficus in Helene's room—the one she bought at her preschool's flower sale and is at least ninety-eight percent dead. That'll make points with Corinne, who is losing her enthusiasm for the fallen leaves and the tiny white bugs that are all over them.

As for Mr. Solway—despite the fact that I've forgotten most of what's happened to me, I feel confident saying he's the coolest person I've ever met. Anyone who could jump onto a moving enemy tank, throw open the hatch, and take it out with a grenade has to be a pretty amazing guy.

Mr. Solway doesn't see it that way. "That's what I did, not who I am. If I'd bothered to think about it, I wouldn't have done it. I'm not that stupid."

The sad part is that Mr. Solway can't find his Medal of Honor. Nurse Duncan thinks it probably got misplaced during Portland Street's big repainting project, and it will turn up sooner or later. But he's convinced he flat-out lost it.

"I haven't been as sharp since my wife died," he tells me. "We never had kids, so we were the whole world to each other. She looked after everything, and I looked after her." He sighs. "You can see which one of us did a better job. When she was gone, that's when my life pretty much ended. This"—a sweep of his arm takes in the room—"is marking time."

I hate it when he talks like that. "Come on, Mr. Solway. You've got a good life here. Plenty of friends."

He glares at me. "Have you ever asked about me around this place? Old ladies on crutches do the hundred-yard dash when they see me coming. I've got my own personal table for one in the dining room. The nurses all call me Mr. Happy Face—they think I don't know, because they assume I'm just as deaf as everybody else in this funny farm."

"I'm getting the sense that, before my accident, I was kind of Mr. Happy Face at my school," I confide to him.

"I could have told you that," he replies. "When you first showed up here, you were just like those other two good-for-nothings—maybe the worst of the three. Sometimes a whack on the head is exactly what a fellow needs."

That's a pretty harsh thing to say to someone with amnesia. But that's just the way Mr. Solway is. He isn't being mean; he's being honest. He's lived a long time and been through a lot, and he doesn't feel like he has to pull any punches. I respect that more than anything.

"That 'whack on the head' cost me thirteen and a half years of my life," I remind him.

"Remembering is overrated," he assures me. "You know that heroic act that earned me that fancy medal? I don't remember one second of it. The only reason I know what happened is from the report my captain filed with headquarters."

"I guess when you get older it's hard to hang on to every detail," I offer.

He shakes his head. "It isn't old age; it's looking into a T-34 tank after a grenade's gone off inside it. Not a pretty sight. That was the medic's explanation, anyway. You block out what you can't face."

"They were the enemy," I say gently. "There was a war on."

"They're always the enemy when they're shooting at you, kid. But a dead man doesn't care what uniform he's wearing. I'm better off forgetting the whole rotten business, medal and all."

That's another thing I have in common with Mr. Solway. We're memory-loss buddies. I wonder if I blocked out what a jerk I used to be because I can't face it. I don't think it's the same thing, though. Besides, *my* lost past has started to come back.

I wouldn't exactly call it a tsunami of recollection. More like that water torture where the blindfolded prisoner feels a drip on his head just often enough to drive him crazy anticipating the next one. I can't even be sure they're real memories—blowing out candles at what could have been one of my birthday parties, a view of the Hollywood sign that might have come from our family trip to California, being crushed under a dog pile of football players—a flashback to one of my sports triumphs?

Who can tell? My mind plays tricks on me. Last night, I had a dream about cherry bombs going off inside a piano, scaring some poor kid half to death, and woke up in a cold sweat.

But when I checked the school yearbook for a picture of Joel Weber, he wasn't the guy in my dream. That was no memory—just the product of a guilty conscience.

My theory is my brain invents fake memories of things I heard about, because I'm trying so hard to remember stuff. I even had a nightmare from the Korean War, and for sure I was never there. I actually saw myself in uniform, climbing up the side of a tank like Mr. Solway did. I yank open the hatch, pull the pin on my grenade, but when the soldiers inside look up at me, I can't bring myself to drop it in on them. I just hang there, not knowing what to do, until the grenade goes off in my hand.

Believe it or not, the impression from before my accident that seems the most vivid is that little girl. Sometimes so much so that I feel like I should be able to reach out and touch the white lace on her blue dress, or the red ribbon in her hair. I have to question whether she's any more real than the dreams. She never moves. She just stands there, not looking at me, but off to the side somewhere.

She must be important, though. She's the one image that was still with me when I woke up in the hospital.

I wonder who she is.

School triggers a few memories too, but they're mostly random images and feelings of déjà vu. There's nothing solid enough to be useful—I still don't really know the faculty, the kids, or the custodians. I'm just now learning my way around a building I've been attending since the sixth grade. I obviously don't remember what a lousy student I was, because my teachers are all so impressed with how well I'm doing now. Some of them seem like they're ready to faint when I actually hand in a homework assignment.

Video club is the one place that's brand-new to me because it actually *is*. We've collected a ton of footage for the yearbook. I'm lagging behind the other members, since most kids run a mile when they see me coming. I always shout, "Brendan sent me!" so they'll know I'm not looking for trouble. Ms. DeLeo wants me to work on my interviewing skills, because my subjects seem so ill at ease. Yeah, no kidding. They're all waiting for me to pull their underwear up over their heads and stuff them into the nearest locker.

At least the video kids are getting used to having me around—except Shoshanna, who hates me for good and always. I can't blame her, even though I have no memory of what Aaron, Bear, and I did to her brother. It's pretty strange to be despised for something that, in your mind, never happened—and to someone it seems like you never met.

She's stopped fighting with me directly. Mostly she makes pointed comments about how the club should have closed up membership while they had the chance. That's unfair, because I'm not even the last to join. Kimmy got here after me, and if I'm a newbie, I don't know what you call her. She doesn't know a camera from a kumquat. For her interview with the head cheerleader, she left the lens cap on, so there was audio and no video. On her second try, she zoomed in so close that all you could see was a mouth talking.

I think Brendan has kind of a crush on Kimmy, because he won't hear anything bad about her. Shooting a mouth but no face is "expressionism" and "lens caps are too analog for a digital age."

Whatever.

Brendan's true love, though, is YouTube. This afternoon, he shows us his latest clip of a tiny goldfish bravely swimming against the pull of a bathtub drain, while electric guitars roar in the background. Just as the struggling creature is about to be sucked away to his doom, a toilet plunger slams down over the drain opening, saving his life.

Brendan pauses the video to scattered applause. "I call it *Plunger Ex Machina*," he announces grandly.

Shoshanna doesn't approve. "You're wasting your time with this stuff. You should be helping me with my entry for the National Video Journalism Contest. It would be a huge boost for the club if we win."

He brushes her off. "The kind of Internet traffic I'm trying to generate isn't going to come from some senior citizen reminiscing about the good old days."

"That depends on who we pick," Shoshanna insists. "Seniors have lived through amazing times and accomplished incredible things. We just have to find the perfect subject—"

Before I realize who I'm talking to, I blurt, "You should talk to Mr. Solway over at Portland Street."

Her angry eyes skewer me. I've contaminated her precious

project with the sound of my voice. Another of my crimes against humanity, like bullying her brother, and not dying when I fell off the roof.

"Who's Mr. Solway?" Kimmy asks.

"A hero from the Korean War. He was awarded the Medal of Honor—that's the highest award any soldier can get."

"And how would *you* know someone like that?" Shoshanna demands. It's obvious she doesn't believe a word out of my mouth.

"I work there—Aaron, Bear, and me. It's our community service for . . ." My voice trails off. She of all people knows exactly what we're doing community service for.

"He sounds perfect," Brendan agrees.

"Maybe I can get him to ride a tricycle through the car wash," Shoshanna retorts icily.

"At least talk to the guy," Hugo prods.

Ms. DeLeo wades in to play peacemaker. "I know you'll find a way to make the school proud," she says to Shoshanna. "And thank you, Chase, for a marvelous suggestion."

Shoshanna's cheeks darken through pink and red to full crimson.

I hope I never hate anybody as much as that girl hates me.

CHAPTER THIRTEEN

SHOSHANNA WEBER

I get it. We're nerds. The video club, I mean.

We *own* it too—take something meant as an insult and be proud of it. Nerd Power. After all, the shoe totally fits. We wouldn't be as happy doing whatever it is the so-called cool people do.

That's how I always looked at it. We are who we are, and we're good with it. I figured the others felt the same way. Who cares what the popular kids think of us?

Was I ever wrong about that! As soon as someone from the A-list showed even the slightest interest in video club, we all went weak in the knees and lined up to love him.

My friends used to act like attention from the cool people meant nothing to them because they never thought they'd get any. But now that they've had a little taste, they're hooked.

Brendan—who was bullied by Chase almost as much as Joel was—has turned into Chase's biggest fan. And none of those sheep can stop raving about Chase's "amazing" suggestion for my National Video Journalism Contest entry.

I can think of a lot of words to describe Chase, and *amazing* isn't any of them. Except maybe that it's *amazing* he isn't in jail.

On the other hand . . . well, that contest *is* important to me, and it's not like I've got a better idea. I did a little research, and the Medal of Honor turns out to be just as special as Chase says it is. Even a broken clock gives the correct time twice a day.

I figure I'll go talk to this Mr. Solway. If he really did win a Medal of Honor, I owe it to myself to check him out.

On the walk over to Portland Street, my phone pings. A message from Joel.

JWPianoMan: Where u?

Shosh466: In town.

JWPianoMan: Hot date?

Yeah, right. With a guy who must be at least eighty. I thumb back:

Shosh466: Video club business.

JWPianoMan: ???

Shosh466: Meeting possible subject for contest video. Korean War hero.

JWPianoMan: Wow, where'd you find him?

I hesitate. I never told Joel that while he's suffering at Melton, Chase has moved in and taken over his spot in the video club. It would only make a miserable situation worse. And I'm definitely not going to admit that Chase put me onto Mr. Solway. I don't like keeping secrets from my brother, but there are some things you just can't say. Maybe, in a few months, if Joel starts fitting in at boarding school and making some friends there—or at least not hating it—I can break the news to him and he won't care so much.

So I message back:

Shosh466: Friend of a friend.

I put away my phone, praying that he doesn't ask for more information. Joel is a cross between a prosecuting attorney and a bloodhound if he gets the idea that you're holding out on him. Especially now, when he's lonely and bored, with nothing better to do than think about home.

At Portland Street, I ask at the desk, and they direct me to room 121. As I make my way through the halls, I get a sense of just how elderly some of the residents must be. My grandfather is seventy-three, and he still Rollerblades every morning. These people are way older than him. A lot of them must be in their nineties, and maybe even over a hundred.

The door of 121 is ajar, so when I knock on it, it swings open.

"Mr. Solway?" I ask tentatively.

A gruff voice announces, "We don't want any."

"I'm—uh—not selling anything." I step farther into the room and get my first view of him. I can't see him directly, since he's facing away from me, watching a news channel on TV. He's short but sturdy, with thick white hair. "I just want to talk to you. I'm in the video club at my school and—"

"You call yourself a governor!" he bellows suddenly at the TV. "You couldn't run a hot dog cart! You're an idiot!"

I keep talking. I do that when I'm nervous. "And there's this national contest where you have to interview a senior citizen who's had an interesting life—"

He turns in his chair and fixes me with his burning gaze. "Do I know you?"

I'm still babbling. "And I heard you were awarded the Medal of Honor in the Korean War—"

He reddens. "Is that what this is about? That medal doesn't make me any more special than a lot of other people who were there. Go interview one of them and leave me out of it."

I'm trying to be reasonable. "Don't you want your story to be told?"

"No. It's my story. It's enough for me to know it."

By now, I've caught sight of the picture of President Truman hanging the medal around a younger Mr. Solway's neck, and I'm convinced that he has to be my subject. "A lot of kids my age don't understand the sacrifices people like you made for our country."

"Don't flatter me, kid. I'm eighty-six years old, and there's precious little left of me to flatter. I don't want to be interviewed. I don't want to be thanked. All I want is for the dining room to stop serving creamed spinach."

I'm completely defeated. The guy is impossible—absolutely determined to stew in his own misery. He almost reminds me of Joel, who is so ticked off at where he ended up that he can't allow himself to try to make the best of it. Because then he'd have nothing to complain about, and complaining is the only thing that keeps him going.

The difference is that Joel has every right to be angry at the curveball life pitched him; this old creep is just plain mean.

I'm about to back out the door in defeat when a familiar voice announces, "Good news, Mr. Solway—I snagged the last prune Danish."

There he is—the Alpha Rat of my family's nightmares, bearing a pastry on a paper plate. He's got a name tag on, proclaiming him to be CHASE—VOLUNTEER.

The change in Mr. Solway is incredible. His crabby glower morphs into a grin that lights up the room. Come to think of it, it makes perfect sense: Who can cheer up a miserable jerk who would never give anybody else the skin off a grape? Only another miserable jerk, someone even nastier and more selfish. The two of them were made for each other.

Then Chase notices me.

"Oh, hi, Shoshanna—" His smile disappears when I glare at him.

"Wait a minute," Mr. Solway exclaims. "Is she your friend, Chase?"

He nods. "We're in video club together. I'm the one who suggested you for her project."

The old soldier thinks it over and comes to a conclusion with a curt nod. "That makes it different. I'd be happy to help the two of you out."

I don't like the sound of that. I don't have a partner for this contest. And even if I did, the last person on earth I'd ever choose would be Chase Ambrose.

But if I say that to Mr. Solway, I'll get kicked out again—this time for good.

I turn furious eyes on Chase. He gazes innocently back and I know that somewhere deep inside, he's laughing at me.

It looks like I have a partner—whether I want one or not.

And I don't.

How am I ever going to explain this to Joel?

CHAPTER FOURTEEN

CHASE AMBROSE

My dad recently bought himself a souped-up Mustang with four hundred horsepower, huge tires, and just enough of a defect in the muffler that it roars like a bulldozer. That's what he drives when he isn't in the Ambrose Electric truck—he won't be caught dead in Corinne's van. And, he assures me, when I'm sixteen, my first lesson will be behind the much-beloved wheel of "the 'Stang."

"I hope not," I tell him, "because I won't be able to make out a single word over the engine noise."

He laughs appreciatively. "You won't be able to hear a police siren either. But you'll be able to outrun one." We pull up in front of my house and he kills the engine so we can hear each other scream.

"Thanks for dinner, Dad. Corinne's a great cook."

"The best."

"Helene's really fun too. I guess we're turning into pretty good friends."

He grimaces. "Because you played princess with her."

"Yeah, well, we were going to have an ultimate fighting match, but we couldn't find an octagon."

Dad doesn't crack a smile. "I guess you never struck me as the kind of kid who'd care whether or not he's 'pretty good friends' with a four-year-old."

I shrug. "She used to be afraid of me. Isn't this better?"

"She wasn't afraid of you, exactly. But you were different then. Tougher. Nobody messed with you. Think of Aaron and Bear. Like that."

I'm having flashbacks of my wonderful toughness—punching and shoving kids, kicking their heels out from under them in the halls. But it's not all bad stuff like that. I remember walking through the school with my shoulders back and my head held high. I remember feeling important and confident and powerful. Maybe some of that came from what a jerk I was, but surely not all of it. I was a star athlete and a state champion. I had a lot of friends. I was *somebody* in this town. It's not a crime to be proud of that.

I reach for the door handle. "Anyway, thanks again, Dad."

"One more thing, Champ," he says quickly. "There's this doctor. He's a sports medicine expert, so he has a lot more experience than that quack Cooperman. I talked to his office and he's willing to take a look at you to give us a second opinion."

"A second opinion?" I echo. "We know exactly what happened to me. What's a second opinion going to do?"

"Get you on the field, where you belong!" he exclaims immediately. "Even Cooperman admits you've recovered. It shouldn't cost you your whole season!"

"Dr. Cooperman explained all that," I remind him. "You know, abundance of caution and blah, blah, blah."

"And if that's the right move, Dr. Nguyen will tell you the same thing. But if it's not, you're throwing away your eighth-grade year, maybe another state championship! Nobody's ever won two in a row—not even me!"

His face is flushed with passion. There's no doubt in my mind that he's one hundred percent sincere. Even more amazing, he's talking about me surpassing what he accomplished on the Hurricanes. Obviously, there's a lot I can't remember, but for him to suggest I might go *beyond* him—that he might be second best after me—that's *huge*!

How could I not see this Nguyen guy? He's a specialist, which means he knows more about sports injuries than anybody—including Dr. Cooperman. If he gives me the okay to play, then nobody can stop me.

"I'll tell Mom," I promise.

"God, no!" he explodes. When I gawk at him, he adds, "We don't want to worry her. She's got enough on her mind. I'll take you to Dr. Nguyen, and when we get the all clear, then we'll find a way to bring it up to your mother."

I don't want to get my hopes up too high. "You mean *if* we get the all clear," I amend.

"Whatever. But I've got a good feeling about this, Champ. You'll have your old life back before you know it."

My old life. I allow my mind to sift through the idea. I'm excited to play football, but what I really crave is the chance to be *me* again. To make up with my best friends and mend fences with the team. Those feelings of self-assuredness and pride won't just come from memories anymore.

It could all happen very soon.

Bear snatches the pass out of the air, hugs the ball close to his body, and executes a lightning spin move around a lady pushing a baby carriage on the sidewalk.

"Watch it!" she barks as the startled baby begins to scream.

"Sorry!" I shout over my shoulder, and we continue along Portland Street, tossing the ball between the three of us.

I'm not back on the team yet, but no one said I couldn't play a friendly game of catch as we make our way to community service.

The "friendly" part is just for us. It doesn't include our fellow pedestrians, who run for their lives when they see us coming.

"Hey, cut it out!"

"Watch where you're going!"

"That's my head you almost took off!"

A ten-year-old kid lets loose a string of obscenities when we knock him off his bike.

"You kiss your mother with that mouth?" Aaron crows gleefully.

Laughing, I haul the kid and his bike upright and turn back just in time to see the ball screaming at my face. At the last second, I reach up and pick it out of the air. *Not bad*, I think to myself. Maybe I really am the star everyone says I used to be.

Aaron and Bear are all power and no finesse. Aaron's even kind of a butterfingers—he's constantly running into the road after the bouncing ball, amid squealing brakes and honks of outrage. But I seem to have some real skills, and what Dad would call good hands.

"Great catch, Ambrose!" Aaron bellows. "Now you see how much the Hurricanes need you."

I grin, but don't tell them about the appointment Dad's going to set up with Dr. Nguyen. I don't want them celebrating something that might not happen if the new doctor doesn't clear me to play.

But he's going to. I can feel it.

When we get to the Portland Street Residence, I spy Shoshanna just stepping in the front door. Luckily, Aaron's looking the other way, and I throw Bear a bullet pass to make sure he doesn't see her. It wouldn't be easy to explain to those guys that she and I are working together.

I don't have a time sheet to sign, so when they head to the office, I make a beeline for Mr. Solway's room. I'll have to catch up with them at some point, but the way they goof off and eat cookies, I've got plenty of time.

I don't feel great about running around behind their backs, but it's easier this way. Why stir things up if I don't have to?

". . . so the colonel is lecturing us on conserving resources and right behind him on the landing strip, the PFCs are unloading the six coolers of pastrami sandwiches we had flown in from San Francisco. And we're praying he doesn't turn around because we sent two pilots over twelve thousand miles, including a stop at the Midway Islands, to get us lunch. We're breaking our arms patting ourselves on the back that we got away with it, when the colonel sniffs the air and says, 'Call me crazy, but I could swear I smell pastrami!'"

I cling harder to the flip-cam so my laughter won't make the picture jump. I can see that Shoshanna, the interviewer, is actually biting the side of her mouth to keep from cracking up. You don't want to do anything to interrupt Mr. Solway. Once he gets started, the stories tumble out, one after another.

It's our third day at Portland Street working with the old soldier, and our best yet. Shoshanna never planned on spending more than a couple of hours here, but neither of us counted on Mr. Solway having so much to say. Most of the time, he's all sarcasm, so it's hard to have a normal conversation with him.

The big difference is Shoshanna, who's a natural interviewer. She's so genuinely interested that she brings out the best in Mr. Solway.

Some of the stories are sad, like losing friends in battle or having to rescue children orphaned by the war. Some are uplifting—the work of medics and nurses, and the incredible heroism of ordinary soldiers. But amazingly, in the middle of all that suffering and violence, a lot of funny stuff happened too. Like the pastrami incident, or the time General MacArthur's laundry was sent to their post by mistake, and they used his silk boxer shorts as party hats on New Year's Eve.

I get the impression that Mr. Solway was the army's version of a class clown, which doesn't really match the cranky old geezer he is now. Or maybe it does—I think of his mistrust of authority figures like doctors and administrators. He saw almost as many of those during the war as he does today in assisted living. After he took out that tank, he spent five weeks in the hospital. He was nearly court-martialed for running an illegal gambling operation. He filled empty IV bags with helium and took bets on balloon races. While he's telling it to Shoshanna, he's roaring with laughter. His face is pink from the joy of the memory.

"I had fifty bucks on the hot water bottle—that was a lot of money in those days—and this crazy Texan threw a hypodermic needle like a dart and brought me down three feet shy of the finish line. I've never been so mad at anybody in my life! But I paid up—at least I was going to until the MPs raided the game, party poopers!"

Engrossed in the story, I nearly miss the twin gasps from the hall. I glance over my shoulder to spy Aaron and Bear standing in the doorway, staring in bewilderment.

Busted.

"Let's take a break, okay?" I set down the camera and join them outside.

"What gives?" Bear demands. "First you come with us to

community service when you don't even have to—that's bad enough! But now you're making a movie about the place?"

"It's for video club—"

"And with Shoshanna Weber?" Aaron cuts me off. "Her stupid family got us sentenced to the Graybeard Motel!"

"Maybe I'm trying to make things right with her," I defend myself. "Maybe if I help her with her project, the family will be in more of a forgiving mood."

"Yeah, that'll work," Aaron snorts. "Listen, man, you might not remember how much the Webers hate our guts, but I do. If it was up to them, we wouldn't be on community service; we'd be on death row. But, hey, it's all good. If you want to spend your time with people who curse the day you were born instead of your true friends—it's not like we can stop you."

I'm torn. On the one hand, I'm not doing anything wrong. Still, I've kind of brought this on myself by covering up the fact that I'm working with Shoshanna. Aaron looks honestly hurt—like I'm stabbing him in the back. And let's face it, he might be kind of right. After all, I didn't have to be so secretive about the video project.

Bear chimes in. "And of all the Dumbledores in this place, why do you have to pal around with that one? If you're looking for relics, this place is like an all-you-can-eat buffet. Why him?"

"We're interviewing him," I try to explain. "He's the most interesting person here. The guy's a war hero!"

They stare at me like I've got a cabbage for a head through

a long, weird silence. Finally, Aaron mumbles, "Yeah, you showed us the picture."

"The way you ignore all the residents here, I figured maybe you forgot."

"Yeah, well, we didn't," Bear snaps. "We know all about Mr. Steinway."

"Solway," I correct.

Aaron is annoyed. "Listen, when you're practicing football three hours a day and doing community service because you *have* to—not because it's your hobby—you've got a lot more on your mind than remembering every old coot's name. Come on, Bear."

"Look who's talking about forgetting," Bear adds resentfully as they head down the hall.

Way to go, Chase, I chew myself out as they round the corner. This is exactly what I was trying to avoid. And now they're ticked off at me. Worse, they feel like they can't trust me anymore.

What next, huh?

When I reenter the room, the first thing I see is Mr. Solway's walker standing against the wall. The old soldier himself is up on his feet, directing Shoshanna, who is pulling a heavy box out of the closet.

"You know," she's saying, "I thought being in the army taught people to be more orderly."

Mr. Solway throws his head back and guffaws loudly. "I'm the exception to that rule. Some of the fellows—to this day, they make a bed so tight you could bounce a quarter off the blanket. Me, I always hated the spit and polish. I promised myself that the minute there was no sergeant around to search for a speck of dust on my boots, I was going to be as messy as I wanted to be."

"Well, in that case," Shoshanna informs him, "this closet is your crowning glory."

Instead of being insulted, the old soldier looks kind of pleased.

I can see it from all the way across the room. There are a few shirts, pairs of pants, and one suit on hangers pushed over to one side. The rest of the space—ninety percent of it—is jam-packed with what can only be described as *stuff*. Picture the entire contents of a house crammed into a tiny four-by-four space. All the things that would end up in the basement, the garage, the attic live in that closet. There are books, Ping-Pong paddles, a broom, a couple of bowling trophies, hip waders and a fishing rod, framed pictures, a weed whacker, ice skates, a three-foot-high oriental vase with a crack up the side, a golf umbrella, a garden gnome, luggage, and cartons of varying sizes. As I cross the room, I get a peek inside the box that Shoshanna dragged out. It contains three replacement furnace filters, jumper cables for a car, and a sterling silver nutcracker set.

It looks like exactly what it is—the things a person collects over eighty-six years. And when that person moves to a place where all the storage space is one little closet, it gets pretty tight in there.

"We've got a lot of great footage of Mr. Solway talking," Shoshanna explains to me from the depths of the collection. "But what we need are some visuals to cut away to—mementos, old photographs, that kind of thing. What do you think?" When we're talking project business, she sometimes slips up and treats me like a fellow human.

"Good idea," I agree.

Mr. Solway peers into another box. "Son of a gun! I was wondering what I did with my thirty-two-piece ratchet set."

I look at him, standing up and walking on his own, even bending over to see inside the carton. It's hard to believe that this is the same Mr. Solway that I first met, struggling on the walker and never even bothering to open the blinds to let some light into his gloomy room.

Maybe when his wife died and he moved into Portland Street, he lost focus because everything in his life used to revolve around her. But now that Shoshanna and I are coming over to work on the video, he's totally different. He wants to present himself well on camera, so he shaves, dresses well, stands straighter, and walks better. According to the nurses, his appetite has improved at mealtimes.

We dig around some more, moving stuff out of the closet and unpacking boxes until the floor is covered in knickknacks. We do find a few things we can use in the video—black-and-white photographs from the barracks in Korea; the Solways' wedding picture in a double frame with one from their fiftieth anniversary; his old military dog tags and another set belonging to a buddy who was killed in the war.

We've got enough, but Shoshanna is like a bloodhound, on her hands and knees in the closet, running her hand along the baseboard.

"What are you doing back there?" Mr. Solway asks. "Drilling for oil?"

She reaches behind a golf bag and draws out a navy-blue velvet jewelry box of an odd triangular shape. Embossed in silver on the lid is the Great Seal of the United States.

"You found my medal!" Mr. Solway exclaims in amazement.

Glowing with discovery, Shoshanna flips open the cover.

The box is empty.

Mr. Solway frowns. "It must have fallen out."

Shoshanna and I give the closet floor a thorough inspection. No medal.

She has a question. "Mr. Solway, when was the last time you wore your medal?"

"In this place?" He's sarcastic. "Lots of state occasions here. Wheelchair races. Canasta games. Colonoscopies—"

"What about before that? Before you moved here?"

He casts her a wry grin. "I get you. *What if the crazy old codger packed up the empty case for a medal he lost twenty years ago?* No, don't apologize. It's a valid question. The answer is I never wore it. Not that I was ashamed of it, but it didn't feel right—like I'd be saying, 'Look how great I am. I've got a better medal than you. Any dimwit can win a Purple Heart.' My wife used to take it out once a year on Veterans Day. And when I refused to wear it, she'd polish it up and put it away again. Maybe one time she misplaced it. She was confused toward the end. It's possible."

He retreats to his easy chair and sits in silence. Talking

about his wife always makes him sad. We quit filming early in order to leave our subject with his memories.

"I love Mr. Solway, but he's pretty weird," Shoshanna says as we cross the lobby, heading for the exit. "He won his country's highest honor and basically ignored it."

"People were different back then," I offer. "You know, more modest."

"Yeah, sure, modest. But to care so little that you don't even bother to open the case to see if the medal's still there? And then hide it in the back of your closet behind a golf bag? You've got to be a real oddball."

We're going through the sliding doors, which might be why she doesn't notice that I stagger for a split second.

Missing medal. Empty case buried under tons of junk. Mr. Solway's medal wasn't lost. It was stolen. Somebody pocketed it and tossed the case where it would be hard to find.

Who would do such a thing? There are plenty of possibilities. Portland Street is a busy place, with a big staff—doctors, nurses, attendants, service people. There were painters in recently. It could have been one of the other residents, or even a visitor.

But as I run my mind over the range of suspects, an image keeps forcing itself in front of my eyes. I see a twenty-dollar bill in Mrs. Swanson's shaky hand. I see greedy fingers snatching it away.

Bear. And Aaron gloating over all the pizza it would buy.

Of course, there's a big difference between twenty bucks and the decoration awarded to a war hero to honor his bravery above and beyond the call of duty. But somebody greedy enough to take money from a confused old lady who thinks she's tipping room service—how could a guy like that pass up the chance to get his hands on something far more valuable?

I must turn pale, because Shoshanna regards me in concern. "Are you okay? You look like you're about to face-plant."

"I'm fine."

I'm *so* not fine, but I keep my mouth shut. What kind of friend am I that I instantly suspect Aaron and Bear of stealing Mr. Solway's medal? What kind of friends are *they* that it's so easy for me to believe they did it?

Two hard questions followed by a third:

What should I do now?

CHAPTER FIFTEEN

BRENDAN ESPINOZA

Of all the video clubs in all the middle schools, she has to walk into mine!

The minute Kimberly Tooley showed up in Ms. DeLeo's room, I was lost. Love at first sight.

For me. Unfortunately, not for her.

I mean, she's in love all right—with Chase.

A few months ago, it would have been easy for me to hate Chase. But he's a different person since his accident. And the more I get to know him, the more I like him.

Now what am I supposed to do? Hate someone I like because of pure jealousy? That's just as unfair as when Chase used to pick on me. Maybe more, since he truly seems to have no idea that Kimberly likes him. How annoying is that? I'd lie down on railroad tracks for an ounce of her attention, and here's Chase, totally oblivious to the fact that she's practically drooling over him! Exactly how hard did that kid fall on his head?

So I've got Kimberly in *my* video club—okay, I don't own it, but I'm the president. It's a golden opportunity for me to make an impression on her. And who's sucking all the air out of the room? Our rising star, Chase.

I've got no one but myself to blame. *I* recruited him. *I* raved about his camera skills. When the others wanted to keep him out, *I* shouted them down. Slowly but surely, they all began to accept and appreciate him. Even Shoshanna isn't quite so anti-Chase anymore. Their project on Mr. Solway is coming out fantastic. I've seen some of the footage, and it's going to blow the judges away. Their biggest problem is they're shooting so much great material that it's going to be impossible to figure out what to cut.

And that opens an opportunity. With Shoshanna and Chase wrapped up in their war hero, and the others focused on the video yearbook, all I have to do is get Kimberly to work with me on a new clip for YouTube. Then she'll start to see me as the famous YouTuber I'm destined to be, not the eighth-grade nerd she finds so much less interesting than Chase.

It's foolproof!

"No," she says.

"Why not?" I wheedle. "It'll be a great chance for you to practice your camera work."

"Is it for the yearbook?"

"It's way better. It's for YouTube. And your name will be right at the top as a coproducer!"

"No," she says again.

In total desperation, I blurt, "Chase is going to be there."

The change is instant. "Really?"

Guess what—she's in. Now all I have to do is convince Chase to sign on with us. Come to think of it, the purpose of this is to turn her off Chase and onto me. I don't think I'm going about it the right way. This whole romance thing is way more complicated than I anticipated.

But when I approach Chase, he's not that enthusiastic either.

"You know, I don't have a lot of free time," he tells me. "Shoshanna and I are really busy with Mr. Solway."

I'm pleading now. "You've got to help me out. Kimberly begged me to take her along, and you know how lousy she is with a camera. If you don't come, the whole video's going to be upside down!"

He sighs. "All right, Brendan. I'll be there."

By now the project is leaving a bad taste in my mouth. Luckily, I have an amazing idea. It's called *Leaf Man*. I know that when Kimberly sees me starring in this, she'll be impressed. It could very well be the video that finally takes me viral.

We meet in the park the next day after school. I've got everything we need—a Morphsuit, Rollerblades, and eleven bottles of pancake syrup. I hand Kimberly camera one and Chase camera two—although I'm pretty sure Chase's footage will be the real video. Anything usable Kimberly shoots will be a happy accident.

I duck behind a tree and take out the Morphsuit. To my dismay, it's *white*. I specifically told Mom to get black! I'm going to look like a bowling pin in front of Kimberly. But it's too late to fix that now.

I put on the suit and the Rollerblades and glide back to Chase and Kimberly. "All right, you guys. Dump the syrup all over me."

If the goal is to get Kimberly to notice me, mission accomplished.

"Why?" she asks, wide-eyed.

I point to the far end of the park to the giant mountain of leaves the gardeners have blown in the corner. "I cover myself in sticky syrup and Rollerblade down the hill into the leaves. When I come out—it's Leaf Man!"

She's bewildered. "Who's Leaf Man?"

"*I'm* Leaf Man! All the leaves are going to be stuck to the syrup, see, and the video will be called *Leaf Man*, so . . ."

Chase takes pity on me. "It's going to be awesome." He opens one of the bottles and pours a thick stream over my head. Even through the Morphsuit fabric, it feels gooey and gross. The things I do for my art. And Kimberly, of course—although that doesn't seem to be working too well.

Eleven bottles later, I'm covered in the stuff . . . and starting to draw flies.

"All right," I say. "Let's do this."

Confession: I'm not the greatest Rollerblader in the world, and I can't get up the hill. I keep rolling back farther than I make it forward. They have to haul me to the top, Kimberly dragging me by the wrists and Chase pushing from behind. We get some strange looks, although nowhere near the number we're bound to attract when we shoot the actual video.

Production is put on hold a few minutes while my camerapeople wash the stickiness off their hands and get into position by the leaf pile. At last, Chase flashes me the high sign, and I ease my weight off the foot brake and sense the slope starting to move me slowly forward.

The *slowly* part doesn't last very long. The acceleration happens much faster than I expected. In a few seconds, I'm hurtling down the path at dizzying speed. Proper Rollerblade form says I should crouch for better balance, but I'm too scared to bend my locked knees. I can actually feel the g-forces forming the syrup on my face into thin streams. With a sinking heart, I realize that this video may go even more viral than I thought—not as *Leaf Man* but as *Kid Breaks Every Bone in Body in Goo-Drenched Rollerblade Stunt.*

Through a brownish film of syrup, I spot Kimberly and Chase on either side of the mountain of leaves, flip-cams pointed at me. At least, Chase's is pointed at me. Kimberly seems to be filming the air above my head. Then they're gone and all I can see is the leaf pile barreling toward me.

I hit the leaves with a *FOOMF* and end up buried at least four feet inside the mountain before my momentum stops. I lie there for a moment, stunned, listening to the muffled sound of Chase laughing from the outside world. It takes a long time to fight my way out of the mess because a lot of the mess is coming with me, stuck by syrup to the Morphsuit. When I rip the leaves off my face, I see that the pile is about a third as big as it used to be, and the sky is dancing with blowing debris.

As soon as I can breathe, I finish the script by thrusting a fist in the air and bellowing, *"Leaf Man!"*

I never quite get the second syllable out because I'm bowled over by a big golden retriever, who climbs on top of me, licking at the syrup. I can already hear the chorus of barking, and I know that every dog in the park is heading in my direction.

At least they'll keep the flies at bay.

I struggle up and try to skate away, but the wheels on my blades are jammed with syrup-soaked leaves. I take three clumsy steps before landing flat on my face, where I'm immediately buried under a canine swarm. I'm gratified to see that Chase is still filming, his hand steady even though he's doubled over with hilarity.

"I don't get it," Kimberly says over the dog-slurping. "Is this supposed to be funny?"

The amazing thing is that after all this, I still like Kimberly just as much as before. Maybe even more.

Love isn't just blind. It's also totally stupid.

CHAPTER SIXTEEN

SHOSHANNA WEBER

Joel is more miserable than ever at Melton Conservatory. I was hoping he'd start to settle in a little better, but it just isn't happening.

He calls home every night and talks to Mom and Dad, and me too, for hours on end. Most of the time he doesn't even complain. He just grills us about everything that's going on in Hiawassee without him, and I can tell he's so homesick it's tearing him in two.

The other night, he Skyped in just to watch me give Mitzi, our cocker spaniel, a bath. Mitzi had gotten loose that afternoon, and when she came home, she was covered in crushed leaves and some kind of syrup or honey. It took three soapings and half an hour with a comb to get her clean. Joel stayed online for the whole thing and helped me talk her through it. He even refused to go down to the dining hall for dinner. This was the kid who formerly wouldn't be in the same room with Mitzi because she made him sneeze.

I don't dare mention my project with Mr. Solway to Joel. What if he asks who I'm working with? I'm not going to lie, but how can I tell him? And he'll see right through me if I try to fudge my answer, as in, "Oh, just some new kid . . ." Twins can read each other, even from miles away.

The hard part is, video club is one of the things Joel asks about the most. I give him updates on the progress we're making with the video yearbook, and provide play-by-play on Brendan's pathetic attempts to get Kimberly Tooley to notice him. These days, that's the only thing that gets a laugh out of Joel. I work very hard not to say anything that might lead him to ask a question I can't give him the answer to.

He comes close a few times:

JWPianoMan: Did u ever look into entering that national video contest?

Shosh466: Tons of homework in 8th grade.

That's what it's come down to between us. I don't lie, but I don't tell the truth either.

It's sad, because my project with Mr. Solway has turned into the biggest thing in my life. We should have been done two weeks ago. We already have so much material that we could cut it off anytime and still have more than we could ever use.

But it goes beyond just the great interviews we're getting. We've really made friends with the old guy. Most of the time, we're barely working anymore. We take him out for walks; he treats us to lunch. We had a picnic once. Chase and I have really bonded with him.

There, I said it. *Chase and I.*

Just like Mr. Solway has become a part of my life, so has the kid that Joel and I call Alpha Rat. To be honest, I hardly ever think of him by that nickname anymore. I want to. I know it's an act of Weber family loyalty. And I'm on board with that. I could give a college-level symposium on all the reasons why Chase used to be the rattiest rat ever to drag his rat tail through the primordial ooze.

That's not the point. There's no question he was ratty *then*. The problem is he isn't very ratty *anymore*. He's like a version 2.0 of himself with all the bad stuff written out of the programming.

He isn't even that bad when he's with Beta and Gamma Rats. They're doing community service at Portland Street, so we run into them here and there. The three of them still act like friends, but there's definitely some kind of tension in the group. I can't tell if it's Aaron and Bear who are wary of Chase, or Chase who is wary of those two. Maybe it's simpler than that: If the biggest jerks form a club, everything starts to fall apart when one of them isn't quite so jerky anymore.

There's only one explanation, and it's about as un-Chase as you can get. He's *nice*. I thought he was showing his inner bully when he pulled the football team off Brendan that time, but I was wrong. I sure haven't seen any other signs of that from him.

The biggest indicator of how much Chase has changed is the way he is with Mr. Solway. The Solways never had kids, so Chase has become almost the grandson the old guy never had. At first, I think Chase was just impressed by the Medal of Honor recipient, but it's gone way beyond that now. As much as

Mr. Solway likes me too, the real bond is between him and Chase. I'll always be "your friend," and, occasionally, when Mr. Solway forgets, "your girlfriend."

The first time he called me that, Chase turned the color of a mature eggplant. I'll bet I was even darker purple than that.

"She's not my girlfriend, Mr. Solway," Chase mumbled in embarrassment. "She's just—" And he clammed up again, because he was about to say *a friend*, but he was afraid I'd get mad at him for that. Back then, I probably would have. I'm not so sure about today.

"We're in video club together," I supplied.

The old guy rolled his eyes. "You keep telling yourself that."

Just because Mr. Solway is no longer the hermit of Portland Street doesn't mean he's all sweetness and light. He's still a pretty crusty guy who speaks his mind and doesn't worry about who might disagree with him. He barks arguments at TV news commentators he believes are "idiots," and watches sitcoms with a straight face to prove that they're not funny. He's convinced that the Hubble Space Telescope is fake, and the pictures it sends back are created in a Hollywood film studio. He's stringing a necklace out of all the gout pills he refuses to take. It's his plan to present it as a going-away present to Nurse Duncan when he drives her so crazy that she quits.

"Come on, Mr. Solway," Chase chides. "You like Nurse Duncan. She's good to you."

"She's incompetent," is the growled reply. "I don't have gout. I just have a sore foot every once in a while. Let's see how much tap dancing she's doing when she's my age."

He's entertaining but he can be exhausting too. Sometimes Mr. Solway even exhausts himself and falls asleep in our faces. When that happens, Chase puts a blanket over him and we tiptoe out.

On this particular day, we decide to grab a snack and screen our video footage. I suggest frozen yogurt at Heaven on Ice—the words are out of my mouth before I remember what happened the last time we were in that place together.

He looks worried, so I add, "I promise not to dump anything over your head."

Heaven on Ice is just a few blocks away. We load up sundaes, pick a corner booth, and start to preview the day's efforts on the flip-cam.

It's good stuff. Mr. Solway is ranting about how the designated hitter has ruined baseball, so we're both holding back laughter as we watch. We already have enough footage for five videos. I can't shake the feeling that we keep going back for more just because we don't want it to end.

Chase is having the same thoughts. "I'm going to keep visiting Mr. Solway even after we finish."

"I'll come with you." My response is instant, even though I had no idea I was going to say that.

"Shosh?"

I look up and there's my mother in line at the register, carrying a small frozen yogurt cake.

Suddenly, an expression of utter horror spreads across her face.

"Mom? What's wrong—?"

Then I realize that she's just recognized the person that I'm with, our heads together as we watch the tiny flip-cam screen. I never told anybody in my family who my partner is for the video contest, so I know how this must seem to Mom: that I'm cozied up, practically cheek to cheek, with the horrible bully who made Joel's life unbearable and forced him out of town.

"It's not what it looks like!" I blurt.

Her expression is carved from stone. "The car's outside. I'll drive you home."

"But, Mom—"

"I said get in the car."

Chase stands up. "Mrs. Weber—"

She's been quiet up to now. But being addressed directly by Chase is too much for her. "How dare you speak to me?" she seethes, her entire body shaking. "Everyone in my family is off-limits to you! If I had my way, you and your filthy friends would be in juvenile hall!"

I speak up again. "This is *my* fault, not his! If you have to blame someone, blame me!"

"I *am* blaming you!" She hustles me out the door, tossing over her shoulder at Chase, "Stay away from my daughter!"

"Can't we talk about this?" I plead.

"Oh, we'll talk about this," she agrees. "Trust me, by the time we're through, your ears will be blistered."

We're halfway home before either of us realizes that she never paid for the frozen yogurt cake.

Mom calls Dad, who actually *leaves work early* to come home and talk to me. It's as if they've discovered I have a secret criminal life—like I'm counterfeiting hundred-dollar bills on a printing press behind the old ski suits in the basement.

He tries to sound reasonable. "We want you to be free to discover who you are. We've never put limits on that—"

"Until now," I finish sarcastically.

"We never thought we *had* to!" my mother explodes. "Look, Shosh, you know us. We don't tell you who to be friends with! But *him*? He's the worst kind of bully—the kind who ruins lives! Your brother's, for one!"

"We're not friends," I defend myself. "At least, we didn't start out that way. Chase is in video club now. Doing my contest entry on Mr. Solway was his idea. I didn't want to say yes, but the old guy is *so perfect*!"

"And it never struck you as suspicious that this boy who made a career of tormenting Joel should suddenly turn his attention to you?" Dad challenges.

"Of course it did! I hate Chase Ambrose! I mean, I hate *that* Chase Ambrose. But he's so different now! He's not a bully anymore. He doesn't remember anything that happened before his accident."

"That's convenient," my father says bitterly.

"I thought so too," I admit. "I was positive he was faking that amnesia stuff. But there's just no way. Nobody's that good an actor. And you know what?" They aren't going to want to hear it, but it needs to be said. "We weren't friends at the beginning, but I think we're kind of turning into friends now. I *like* the new Chase."

My mom recoils—honestly. Like I just slapped her.

"Your brother," she begins, her voice shaking, "is completely unhappy, attending a school he hates, instead of at home, living the life he's entitled to, and the reason is that boy you're so quick to defend. I don't know if he's changed and I don't care. The person he *was* broke up this family. What he did to Joel is unforgivable. That means he can never be forgiven."

Dad glares at me. "I'll bet you haven't told Joel who you're buddy-buddy with these days. How would you ever explain that to him?"

That hurts, because he's exactly right.

"Fine," I confess. "I never said anything to Joel. Well, maybe I should have."

"You can't be serious!" my mother exclaims. "What possible good could come of that?"

An idea is forming in my head. Kind of a wild idea, but it's making more and more sense the longer it sits there. "You said it yourself—Joel's lost at boarding school. I think he's more unhappy than he ever was when he was here being bullied."

"And whose fault is that?" Mom demands. "Your new 'friend,' that's who!"

"Can we just talk about Joel for one second, and leave everybody else out of it? He's so depressed at Melton—and maybe he doesn't have to be."

"What are you saying?" my father asks.

"Chase bullied Joel to the point where he had to get out of town," I explain. "But *that* Chase doesn't exist anymore. What if we're keeping Joel at boarding school for nothing?"

They stare at me.

"You mean bring him home?" Mom breathes.

"The reason for him to be somewhere else doesn't exist anymore," I insist. "Chase has *changed*. Aaron and Bear are still jerks, but Chase was always the ringleader. I'm not saying it'll be perfect, but Joel should be here. Joel *wants* to be here! And I'm pretty sure he *can* be here."

I brace myself, expecting them to go off on me: I'm crazy; I'm dreaming; I'm gambling with my brother's life.

Instead—dead silence.

At last, my father finds his voice. "What if you're wrong?"

I have no answer. I only know that I want my brother back. I've wanted it since the day he left for Melton.

Shosh466: Joel—we've got to talk.

CHAPTER SEVENTEEN

JOEL WEBER

The piano is out of tune.

Actually, my whole life is out of tune, but the piano is worse.

I couldn't stand Melton, but everything there was always in tune. It had to be. All the kids had perfect pitch; the instruments were maintained at the highest level; even the wrought-iron gate outside the faculty building squeaked a perfect B-flat. I have perfect pitch too, so I know.

I'm proof that just being *qualified* to attend a musical conservatory doesn't mean you should go there. I love the piano, but not enough to care about it the way people do at a school like Melton. I want to use it to make music, not mind meld with it. There, it's never enough to *play* an instrument. You have to live it, breathe it, taste it, compose for it, understand it inside and out. You even have to empathize with it, like it's another person. Honest.

I hated it. I hated living in a dormitory and sharing a bathroom with eleven other guys. I hated my roommate, and his violin, and his asthma, and the whistling sound he made when he slept—D above high C.

But what I hated most about Melton was the reason I had to go there. To be fair, it wasn't Melton's fault that I was forced out of my own home by three morons. Or that even though everyone knew those three were juvenile delinquents, I was the one who had to suffer.

And now I'm supposed to believe that the leader of the three, Alpha Rat, is a good guy because he fell on his head.

Fine. Whatever gets the job done. I'm home, and an out-of-tune piano is a small price to pay for it.

I'm back where I belong. I'm happy. But . . .

Be careful what you wish for. At Melton, I missed Mitzi so much it was almost a physical pain. That dog drives me crazy. I know she's glad to see me, but she won't leave me alone. I'm always covered in dog hair, which makes me sneeze. And when I kick her out of my room, she lies just outside the door, whining. F-sharp.

My parents are so guilty and conflicted about what happened that they're smothering me. They wait on me hand and foot like I'm helpless. And while it's great to be back with Shosh, she's giving me an uneasy feeling. For one thing, she has entirely too much to say about a certain Alpha Rat.

"Chase thinks Brendan is going to break his neck shooting a YouTube video . . ."

"Mr. Solway threw Jell-O at Chase for letting him win at arm wrestling . . ."

"Chase kept the camera steady while Hugo interviewed the school bus driver—even when they went over the railroad tracks . . ."

I blow my stack. *"Chase says, Chase says,"* I mimic savagely. "Chase has said enough for one lifetime!"

She's patient and understanding. That's another annoying thing. Why does everyone have to be so patient and understanding? One of the perks of living at home should be arguing with your family.

"Wait till you see him at school on Monday. You won't believe how different he is."

"I don't care how different he is," I say honestly. "I don't plan to have anything to do with the guy."

"But you're going to have to deal with him sooner or later," she reasons. "You're coming back to video club, right? Chase is part of that now."

"Good for him."

Her expression turns sympathetic. "I get it. You're nervous."

Well, obviously I'm nervous. I haven't set foot in that school for months and my memories from then are not good. There's something about being bullied that you could never explain to someone who hasn't had it happen to them. It's worse than the sum of the rotten things that are done to you. Even when no one is bothering you, you're still under attack because you're dreading the next strike, and you know it can come from anywhere, at any time. You get so paranoid that with every single step you're half expecting the floor to yawn open and swallow you whole. It got to the point where the only place I felt safe was at the piano. Until the night the piano blew up in my face, and there was no safe place anywhere.

That was my all-time low, and I forgive Mom and Dad for deciding Melton was the answer. I'm a little better now—but only because Melton was so lousy that even coming back to this is an improvement. When a bunch of jerks see you as a victim, that's on them. But when it goes on so long that it's how you see yourself, it's very hard to climb out of that hole.

The hole seems deeper on Monday morning, when Shosh and I get out of the car, and Hiawassee Middle School is right there. I know bricks and concrete are incapable of evil intent, but I can't shake the feeling that the building itself is out to get me.

Dr. Fitzwallace reached out to my parents last week. He offered to meet with me this morning before homeroom. I said no, I'd just print my class schedule at home. I think he wants to reassure me that he has my back. Big deal. He had my back before, and what good did it do? Short of a secret service bodyguard, there's no way to protect anyone one hundred percent. Sooner or later, you're always going to end up in a lonely hallway or a deserted locker room.

Shosh rounds on me. "You ready for this?"

I'm not ready, but I nod. Then we're in, surrounded by all those kids. I forgot the thrum of a school this big—a chaotic buzz of sounds, too many to assign a single note to, or even a whole chord.

A handful of faces turn my way, registering surprise at my return. I hear the occasional whispered, "It's him!" or "Joel's back!" or "You know, the guy whose piano exploded." I catch a couple of kindhearted looks, and even a hostile one from a big kid who must be a football player. Mostly, though, nobody sees me at all—or, worse, they never noticed I was gone. I think that makes me madder than anything else. I went through the worst part of my life—was bullied so badly I had to leave town—and it never popped onto most people's radar screens. That baloney from guidance counselors about how we're supposed to be "a community"—yeah, right. This is how bullies like Chase Ambrose get away with what they do—because their victims are invisible.

Speaking of bodyguards, Shosh thinks she's mine, because she stays glued to my side. Add that to a list of humiliations that doesn't need padding—my sister is convinced she has to fight my battles for me.

"Don't you have to get to homeroom?" I ask her, fighting to keep exasperation out of my voice.

"Oh, I figured I'd stay with you, just for today. I haven't seen Mr. O'Toole in a while—"

I interrupt her. "Go away, Shosh."

She looks worried. "Are you sure?"

"No," I reply honestly. "But you can't hang off me forever. What happens when I have to go to the bathroom?"

"Well, I figured I could wait outside—"

"Go away," I repeat.

Classes are okay, I guess. No different than Melton. Math is math, regardless of whether or not you're learning it from a world-class French horn player. A few kids ask where I've been. Those who know have questions about what boarding school is like.

Brendan Espinoza updates me on his YouTube career, and I congratulate him on *Leaf Man*, which is up to over four thousand views. Not exactly viral yet, but his biggest audience so far. He tells me about video club—Kimberly Tooley is a member, although she never struck me as the type. He talks about her a lot, so I suspect he has some kind of crush going on.

"The biggest news is your sister's entry for the National Video Journalism Contest," Brendan enthuses. "We've been screening the footage and it's awesome. They're just doing the editing now—Shoshanna and—" He falls silent.

"Yeah. I know who her partner is."

"Joel, you're not going to believe how different he is. It's like he split open his head when he fell off the roof, and they put in a new brain!"

"So I've heard." Bad enough I have to listen to Shosh singing Alpha Rat's praises. It never occurred to me that the entire video club would turn out to be fans too.

I pass by Chase in the hall once, and the sight of his face nearly makes me jump out of my skin. But here's the thing: He looks right through me like I'm not even there. Maybe he really does have amnesia and doesn't recognize me.

Well, I recognize him. He's the jerk who did his best to ruin my life last year.

I have no choice but to run into Beta and Gamma Rats. They're in my Spanish class seventh period.

"Look who came crawling home to Mommy," Bear sneers at me.

I'm paralyzed. It's worse than my near miss with Chase in the hall, because it proves that nothing has really changed. Are these my only two choices—this or Melton?

Aaron grabs Bear's arm and drags him to a seat in the back row. "Leave it, man. You want to get in even more trouble thanks to this loser?"

Those two are doing community service over the cherry bombs in the piano. Maybe that'll buy me a little peace.

What I dread the most is the part I used to look forward to—video club. When I was at Melton I practically ached for it. It was the symbol of everything I was missing out on because I'd been exiled. But now all I can think of is that I'm going to come face-to-face with *him*.

When I get to Ms. DeLeo's room, the lights are out and all eyes are on the Smart Board. I assume that this is my sister's famous video project, and the old guy on the screen is that Mr. Solway I've heard so much about. He's describing a scene from the war, and everybody is completely enthralled.

Ms. DeLeo notices me first and pauses the video. She comes over to the doorway to greet me. "Joel—it's so good to have you back."

They crowd around me—all the members. There are a couple of new faces, like Kimberly, but most of them are old friends. It's a nice welcome. I can't enjoy it, though, because I know *he's* there, hanging back, waiting his turn.

Shosh performs a formal introduction—like I don't know the guy who turned my life into a horror show. But of course, it isn't for *me*; it's for him.

"Chase, I don't think you remember my brother, Joel."

He looks ten times more miserable than he ever made me. "I don't even know what to say to you," he begins in a voice I barely recognize as his arrogant Alpha Rat bravado. "I have no memory of any of the things I did to you. And I can't undo them. But I want to tell you that I'm really, *really* sorry."

Up until this moment, I had no idea how I'd react to meeting Chase Ambrose again after all these months. Now I know. I completely believe that he has amnesia and can't recall the stuff that happened between us. I believe that he's changed, and that he honestly regrets what he did to me.

And I know something else: It doesn't make any difference. None. Zero. Zilch.

I still hate his guts.

CHAPTER EIGHTEEN

CHASE AMBROSE

. . . It is the finding of this court that the three juveniles, Chase Matthew Ambrose, Aaron Joshua Hakimian, and Steven Beresford Bratsky, acted recklessly and with malice, not merely destroying property, but creating chaotic circumstances that could have endangered the public safety. Further, this is not an isolated incident; it is part of a pattern of intimidation and misbehavior toward others. Therefore, it is this court's decision that the aforementioned juveniles perform community service until such time as their caseworker concludes that this destructive behavior has been corrected . . .

"Hi, Chase!"

When the hand grasps my shoulder, I practically jump out of my skin, scaring poor Brendan halfway back to the breakfast line in the cafeteria. My head has been spinning all morning. Dad asked for my birth certificate so he could set up the appointment with Dr. Nguyen. I finally found it in Mom's desk. But that's not all I found. I also stumbled on a copy of the court paper sentencing Aaron, Bear, and me to community service.

"What's wrong?" Brendan asks in concern. "You look like you've just seen the zombie apocalypse and it's coming this way."

How can I explain it? It may not be the zombie apocalypse, but it's just as creepy. The judge's words have been burning themselves into my brain: *pattern of intimidation . . . zero remorse . . . pathway to criminality if left unchecked . . .*

I didn't realize how bad it was.

Oh, sure, the flashbacks keep coming. I remember the wide berth kids gave me when I got back to school after the accident—and continue to give me to this day. The general sentiment that Hiawassee Middle School—and maybe the whole world—would be a better place without me. I'm a pretty heavy presence here. And since I've done nothing in my new life to earn that reputation, it's safe to say that it comes from the secret history amnesia erased—from the thirteen years before I fell off the roof.

Up until a couple of weeks ago, my four-year-old half sister treated me like a Sasquatch that wandered into her life—an unpredictable and dangerous beast. And her mother—an adult—wasn't much more comfortable around me.

Aaron and Bear aren't exactly choirboys, so it's safe to assume I wasn't either. But in spite of the rough way they treat other people, they always have my back. That's loyalty—a *good* quality.

Isn't it?

I close my eyes and see the empty velvet case from Mr. Solway's closet.

"Brendan, how bad was I?" I blurt.

An English muffin rolls off his tray and hits the floor.

"What are you talking about?" he stammers. "*Leaf Man* never could have happened if it wasn't for you."

"I mean *before*," I press. "The old Chase."

"Who cares?" he insists. "You were really different then."

"I know I was different. Different how? Did I ever do anything to *you*?"

After a long silence, Brendan runs a finger across his right eyebrow. When I look close, I realize there's a scar there, partly hidden, about half an inch long.

My heart leaps into my throat. "I did that?"

"I was leaning over the drinking fountain. You came by and shoved me in the back of the head. Three stitches."

"Brendan"—my voice is husky—"I'm so sorry."

"You know the worst part?" he goes on. "You just kept walking. You never even bothered to turn around. No follow-up. That's how nothing it was. That's how nothing *I* was."

I can't speak. I think of Aaron and Bear—our loyalty. It kind of doesn't mean as much as I thought it did.

"Anyway," Brendan tells me, "like I said, you're different now. I'll catch you later in video club."

I watch him walk away. I don't know what I'm so broken up about. I haven't learned anything new today, not really. The stuff in the court document—old news. I smell it in every corner of this school. And even if I needed confirmation, it's right there in Joel Weber's eyes.

Fear. Real fear.

It hits me that no matter how different I am—no matter

how much the video club accepts me, or even Shoshanna does—I'll never be able to erase the Chase Ambrose who could strike terror in an innocent kid's heart.

Aaron, Bear, and I must have been no strangers to that look when we were turning Joel's life upside down. I guess having the power to torture another person made us feel like big men. Especially when we picked somebody smaller and weaker, who was into music instead of sports.

And believe it or not, right now, I'm more scared of Joel than he ever was of me. Because if I see that fear in his face again, I don't know if I can handle it.

In spite of all that, Shoshanna and I are getting along better every day. She doesn't hold it against me that her brother thinks I'm the devil. Maybe the turning point was when we were in Heaven on Ice together and she didn't feel the need to dump a giant sundae on my head. The important thing is, we're good.

She's promoted me to full co-creator of our video project on Mr. Solway, which is well into the editing stage. It's coming out fantastic. Editing has been tough, since we have so much great footage. It's practically painful to decide what to cut. We even argue about it, sometimes change each other's minds. It's a real partnership.

Although we're done shooting, we still visit Mr. Solway a lot. On the way, Shoshanna stops at her house to back up our project on her computer. She's really paranoid that the school network will crash and we'll lose our edited footage. So she's constantly saving everything on a memory stick.

It goes without saying that I'm not allowed into the Weber home. We don't actually talk about it. It's just understood that I wait outside while she runs in to do the data transfer.

One afternoon, I'm standing there, hoping Shoshanna's mom doesn't glance out the window and turn the sprinklers on me, when I hear music coming from the house. It's piano, and I realize this must be Joel, Hiawassee's musical prodigy. Obviously, it isn't the first time I've heard him play. Aaron, Bear, and I were in the auditorium to watch our firecrackers go off, so we must have experienced at least a little of his music. But it's my first time in this new life.

He's *amazing*. And not just because he plays fast without making mistakes. The notes flow like a river—speeding up, slowing down, changing in tone and texture. It's almost as if the piano is singing. I wish I knew more about music so I could really appreciate it.

I'm crossing the lawn almost without realizing I'm putting one foot in front of the other. I'm following the sound, which seems to be coming from a side window. Before I know it, I'm at the bushes, peering inside. There's Joel, seated at a baby grand, lost in his performance. I'm almost overcome with shame. We took this kid's talent and made him a target because of it.

When the attack comes, I'm totally caught off guard. A supernova of blond fur launches itself at me, clamping its paws around my leg and burying its teeth in the denim of my jeans. With a cry of shock, I stagger back, toppling into a large barberry bush. As I go down, my face and arms are ripped to shreds by the stiff wooden branches and tiny thorns. The dog is smart enough to jump off before I hit the bush. It stands at the edge of the flower bed, yapping at me.

The music stops and Joel appears in the window. When he spots me lying in the hedge, his eyes widen in shock.

"It's not what you think!" I blurt, even though the window is closed and he probably can't hear me. To Joel, this must look like his former tormentor is at it again, stalking him in his own home. How I could be so stupid?

I try to get up out of the hedge, but every time I move, I get scratched and tangled even more. Plus, that agitates the dog, who starts howling.

A moment later, Mrs. Weber marches across the lawn, tossing over her shoulder, "You must be mistaken, Joel. There's no way Chase Ambrose—" She spies me then and falls silent.

Joel is next. "See? I told you! It's him!"

I try to explain. "I'm just waiting for Shoshanna. We're going to visit Mr. Solway."

"And that's a reason to skulk in our bushes?" Mrs. Weber demands icily.

Technically, I'm doing more bleeding than skulking. But I just say, "I heard the music. And then the dog—"

"Mom?" Shoshanna's voice. "What's going on?"

Shoshanna backs up my story, which, according to Mrs. Weber, is the only reason they're not calling the cops. The two of them drag me out of the hedge, which is even more painful than going in.

"Good dog, Mitzi," is Joel's comment.

I turn to Mrs. Weber. "I'm sorry for the disturbance. I came closer to hear the music, and when the dog attacked, I fell in the bushes." I add to Joel, "You're really good."

He doesn't answer.

His mother looks me over critically. "You're bleeding." And then, "I guess we can't let you walk around like that."

She drags me into the kitchen and washes all my cuts and scratches with antiseptic. The good news is Mitzi's bite didn't break the skin. The bad news is every thorn and branch did. It's the worst agony I can remember since I fell off the roof, and I can't shake the feeling that Mrs. Weber is loving supplying it.

It's the first time I've ever seen Joel smile. Even Shoshanna is grinning a little, although she tries to disguise it as sympathy.

I don't know what's worse—the pain or the reason they're enjoying watching me suffer.

The next time I'm outside the Weber house, waiting for Shoshanna to back up our work, I keep my distance.

Joel's playing the piano again. I hear it, and I can actually see him at the keys through that side window. He glances up, spots me, and gets to his feet.

I'm thinking, *Oh, man, I'm in trouble now. He's going to sic the dog on me again. Or worse, his mom.*

Then he does the last thing I ever expected. He reaches over, opens the window, and goes back to his practicing.

If I didn't know better, I'd swear he wants me to listen.

At school, lunch is turning into the most stressful part of my day. I've been alternating my cafeteria time—one day at the football table with Aaron, Bear, and the Hurricanes, and the next across the lunchroom with the video club. I take a lot of flak from the team, who can't understand me hanging out with "Dork Nation." I realize the players joke around a lot, but it's starting to sound less and less like joking.

Even when I'm with the video club, it's awkward because Joel's there. We're not friends, but we both run with the same crowd. Usually, I sit at one end of the table, and Joel sits on the opposite side. One day, though, he comes late, and the only seat left is right next to me. At first, I think he's going to bolt for the far end of the cafeteria to make a statement that he'd rather eat in another zip code than sit beside me. And he does hesitate a little. Eventually, though, he gives in and sets his tray down next to mine.

Everybody else is looking at us like there's about to be a major war, but nothing happens. Still, a couple of days later, the others make sure there's a spot for Joel nice and far from me.

None of this escapes the watchful attention of Aaron and Bear.

"I get that you hang out with the video dweebs now," Aaron tells me. "But him? Joel Weber? It's thanks to him that we got put on community service!"

"Yeah, and we never did anything to him," I retort sarcastically.

"Okay, fine," says Bear. "But how were we supposed to know he was going to go crying to Mommy?"

"We booby-trapped his piano in an auditorium full of people!" I bark. "I think his mommy would have noticed without him ratting us out!"

"All right, you made your point," Aaron soothes. "It wasn't the nicest thing to do. And we're paying the price for it, aren't we? It's over—forget it!"

"And why Joel, huh?" I go on. "I know you think all the kids at this school who don't play football are either dweebs, wimps, or losers, but how's he different from everybody else? Because he's small? Because he's talented?"

Bear explodes. "Why don't you ask yourself? *You're* the one who picked him! You *used* to be a fun guy, or did you forget that too? We did what we did because it was fun, and the more Weber lost his mind, the funner it was. *Especially to you.* Did it feel great when we heard he was going to that other school? No. But by then we were headed for the Graybeard Motel, so who cared where they sent him?"

I can feel the color draining from my face. That might be the closest I'll ever get to understanding how my brain worked before the accident.

I may not like it, but it's me.

⟵ X ⟶

That afternoon, Shoshanna and I finish the final edit on our entry for the contest. We've titled it *Warrior.* Neither of us can wait to play it for Mr. Solway, but we make the usual stop at the Weber home for Shoshanna to back up our work.

Like always, I wait on the lawn while Shoshanna heads into the house. She pauses in the doorway and tosses a look over her shoulder.

"Aren't you coming?"

A million questions whirl through my head. Did I hear right? Is she kidding? Will her mom kill me? Her brother? Her dog?

Yet somehow I know that if I ask any of them, I'll spoil it, and the opportunity will be lost forever. So I follow her into the house.

Mrs. Weber sees me first. She stares at me for a second and then goes back to the book she's reading. In the living room, Joel is at the piano as usual. He glances up at me, and the music comes to a momentary halt. He takes a long hard look and then goes back to his concerto.

I'm not sure why, but I feel an odd surge of emotion, and have to swallow hard a couple of times.

Even Mitzi wags her tail.

CHAPTER NINETEEN

BEAR BRATSKY

When the announcement comes that there's an assembly, we're all psyched. Why wouldn't we be? It's like a Get Out of Jail Free card for a whole morning of classes. What's the assembly about? Who knows? Who cares?

In the auditorium, the big screen is set up. That means they'll be turning the lights out. The perfect chance to catch a nap for a guy who was playing video games until three last night.

Aaron is way ahead of me. He drapes himself into his seat, his legs dangling over the back of the chair in front of him, his arms spread out wide. I fight my way in beside him and we wrestle for position.

"Hey," exclaims the loser in the row ahead of us—the one with Aaron's size 14 construction boot hanging over his shoulder. But when he sees who he's talking to, he gets real quiet real fast. He and his friends wander off, looking for someplace else to sit.

I flake out next to Aaron.

"Wake me up when it's over," he mumbles, already half-asleep.

"You're the one who's going to be waking *me*," I retort, and we exchange a few rabbit punches before settling in for the big snooze-fest.

Then comes the surprise: The whole purpose of this assembly is so we can congratulate Chase Ambrose and Shoshanna Weber for the amazing video they made for some stupid contest or other. That's all I need—to watch the principal and the teachers lining up to worship the kid who used to be just a guy like me until he fell on his head and suddenly became smart.

It gets worse. We're not just going to worship the video; we're going to watch it—all forty minutes. Well, forget sleeping now. I'm too ticked off. Even Aaron is sitting bolt upright, staring in outrage at Ambrose and the Weber chick onstage.

The video starts. That's when my head really explodes. The thing is called *Warrior*, and it's about that geezer Solway, the meanest old Dumbledore in the entire Graybeard Motel! No wonder the two of them spent so much time with the guy.

Beside me, I can practically see steam coming out of Aaron's ears. "It's not enough for him to make us look like jerks by doing community service when he doesn't have to," he seethes. "No, he has to make a documentary about the place so he can brag to the whole world! And with Shoshanna Weber—from the same family that got us put on community service in the first place. And I thought that guy was my friend!"

"But Solway?" I demand. "What's up with that?"

"Yeah," he agrees. "A whole museum full of ancient fossils and they have to pick the nasty old crab who complains to the nurses if his cookie is off center on the plate."

"That's not what I mean and you know it," I hiss. "Why him, huh? Not just any old Dumbledore. Solway. No way that's a coincidence."

"Chase doesn't know anything about that," Aaron reminds me. "He's got amnesia."

"*If* he's got amnesia," I put in darkly. "Sounds a little convenient to me."

"Well, he's got amnesia enough to forget that he's our boy," Aaron says bitterly.

I nod. "He used to play football. Now he doesn't. He says he's coming back—but I think he's just stringing us along. He's partnered up with a *Weber*, and he's even getting buddy-buddy with *Joel* Weber. He's making it impossible to get along with him. He acts like he's changed, but he's really just cutting us out."

On the screen, there's a close-up photo of a gleaming Medal of Honor. In the voice-over, Shoshanna explains that this isn't the actual medal Mr. Solway received. Mr. Wonderful Solway isn't just a hero; he's modest too. He never wore the dumb thing because he didn't want people to feel bad that they don't have one. And over the years, he forgot where he put it.

"Yeah, right," I mutter.

"Shhh!" Aaron hisses.

When it's finally over, Ambrose and the Weber chick get a five-minute standing ovation. That burns me up, since I know for a fact that the other kids were just as bored as I was. They bring the whole video club up there, because they helped. Ms. DeLeo reads out a letter from the head of the Graybeard Motel thanking the filmmakers for their awesomeness and the school for having such awesome students. Puke.

Aaron and I are sentenced to go to that place three days a week until we're practically old enough to check in there, and what do we get for it? Yelled at, that's what—by nurses and Dumbledores both. And Chase—who's worse than us—gets a love letter from the director.

I've never been so happy to get back to a classroom.

"We can't just do nothing about this," I plead to Aaron as he takes the desk next to me. "He's walking all over us, and we're letting him."

For the very first time, he doesn't look at me like I'm crazy.

"I've got an idea how we can jog his memory. You know, remind him who his real friends are."

CHAPTER TWENTY

BRENDAN ESPINOZA

Leaf Man wasn't the hit I was hoping for, even though it got a lot of YouTube views. For something to go viral, it has to reach a kind of critical mass, where suddenly everybody is talking about it. Poor *Leaf Man* just didn't have enough legs for that.

The bummer is, as great as it was, *Leaf Man* set me back big-time with Kimberly. She's still nice to me, but it might be that she feels sorry for me because she thinks I'm crazy. I'm coming to the conclusion that our senses of humor aren't very compatible. That doesn't mean *we* aren't compatible, just that we probably won't like the same books, TV shows, movies—that kind of stuff.

Besides, she's still totally moonfaced over Chase, so compatibility isn't really an issue right now. The fact that she barely even notices me—that's an issue.

Anyway, I've got an idea for a new video, and this one's going to knock her socks off. It doesn't depend so much on humor as creativity and special effects.

It's called *One Man Band*. Picture this: the Hiawassee music room. The camera films me pretending to play every instrument in the orchestra in front of a green screen. Then I use the video-editing program to superimpose those images onto the various seats on the band risers, until I've got a whole orchestra—and they're all me. Presto—*One Man Band.*

Joel helps me reserve the room for Thursday after school. The music department is so thrilled to have their star back that Mrs. Gilbride would have promised him her firstborn child. Besides, he's known to be a good kid. It's not like he's going to trash the risers or anything like that.

Unfortunately, Chase isn't available to work the camera. He has to take a social studies test he missed due to a follow-up appointment with his falling-off-the-roof doctor. This might be a blessing in disguise because a) Joel volunteers to fill in, and he's a pretty good cameraman, and b) Mrs. Gilbride wouldn't let Chase anywhere near her instruments, amnesia or no. She's still mourning that piano like it was donated to the school by Beethoven himself. Also, c) Kimberly is always a little distracted when Chase is around. Maybe that's why she didn't get the humor in *Leaf Man*. Now, with Chase away writing that test, she'll be able to concentrate on me.

I want to rent a tuxedo, since those orchestra guys really put on the Ritz. My mom won't spring for it, though. So I do the best I can. I take the light gray suit I wore to this kid's Bar Mitzvah and paint it with shoe polish. My white shirt has a bit of a stripe in it, but I'm pretty sure it won't show up on camera. There'll be a lot of me, but luckily, we'll all be pretty small. I borrow a bow tie from my dad to make the whole ensemble more tux-like.

When I come out of the bathroom, all dressed up, on

Thursday, Kimberly wrinkles her nose—a very cute look for her, by the way.

"Dude—you stink! What did you do, take a bath in Magic Marker?"

"It's shoe polish," I explain. "It's not me; it's my clothes. I had to improvise the formal wear."

"Why can't you wear normal clothes?"

"Because an orchestra dresses fancy."

"But you're not in an orchestra."

Well, if she doesn't pay any attention to me, it shouldn't come as a surprise that she doesn't read my texts either. On the way to the music room, I get her up to speed on *One Man Band.*

Her comment is: "You're dripping black gunk on the floor."

"Really?" Uh-oh. There's a trail of shoe polish splatters all the way down the hallway. Too late to worry about that now. Once the video is in the can, I'll do my best to clean up after myself. I think rubbing alcohol works on that stuff. Or maybe nail polish remover.

Joel is waiting for us inside the music room. He's already put up the video club's green screen and set out all the instruments we're going to need. The flip-cam is mounted atop a tripod—another reason why we don't need Chase's steady hand. Joel's got some extra lights plugged in with a spaghetti of power cords. We're ready to roll.

For music, I've chosen a full orchestral version of "For He's a Jolly Good Fellow," performed furiously in triple time. I'll add that in during the editing stage, but I play it on my phone during filming so I'll have the timing right while I'm doing my thing with the instruments. It's not such a big deal with the small stuff—trumpet, clarinet, sax, flute, piccolo. But for violin and the string family, it's important that my bow should be moving to the right tempo. That goes double for the trombone, the kettledrums, and especially the cymbals. If I go crash, then there'd better be a real crash.

"I know this song," Kimberly comments after the music has been playing in an endless loop for at least twenty minutes of shooting. "How come you picked such a lousy song?"

We're in the home stretch: bassoon, French horn, and tuba.

The tuba is last. I stare at it. It's the marching band kind, where you climb into the middle of it, and it's all around your body like a python.

"Wait a minute," I protest. "Where's the regular one?"

"Dented," Joel replies. "Somebody dropped it down the stairs and it's out getting fixed. So it's this one or nothing."

Well, you can't have an orchestra without a tuba. I squirm in and struggle to my feet. I swear the thing weighs more than I do. I'm no Hercules, but the kid who plays this in the marching band is a four-foot-eight-inch sixth-grade girl. How does she lift it, much less have the breath left over to blow into it?

Kimberly is regarding me a little dubiously, so I give her my most confident look and announce, "Piece of cake." It comes out like I'm straining to pass a kidney stone. Not the effect I was reaching for.

I put my lips to the mouthpiece and nod to Joel to start filming the final shot. The camera comes on.

The double doors are kicked open, and before I can react, a tidal wave of white foam fills my field of vision. It hits me full in the face. It wouldn't normally be enough to knock me over. But with the heavy tuba bell suspended above my head, I overbalance and go down like a stone. There's a loud clang as the brass of the instrument strikes the metal edge of the riser.

I hear a gasp of horror from Joel, and soon I understand why. When I roll out of the stream of foam, still wrapped in the tuba, I see Aaron Hakimian and Bear Bratsky, each armed with one of the school's big silver fire extinguishers, spraying down the room and everything and everybody in it.

"Go away!" Joel pleads in a quavering voice.

Aaron laughs a nasty laugh. "Well, if it isn't the loser. I don't think we ever welcomed you back to school. How rude of us!"

"Welcome home, loser!" bellows Bear, and blasts a jet of foam, covering Joel from head to toe.

I turn to Kimberly, who's standing there and, of all things, *giggling*. At long last, the girl has found something funny in one of my videos. She thinks it's part of the plan and doesn't even notice we're under attack.

"Go get help!" I bark at her.

"Yeah, get help," snorts Bear. "Why don't you call your friend Chase?"

That makes sense to me. He's the only one with half a chance of taking on these two. "Get Chase!" I yell at Kimberly.

Aaron laughs cruelly. "And you're supposed to be *smart*! Who do you figure sent us here, genius?"

"You think Chase doesn't remember the loser who got him put on community service?" Bear adds.

"Go!" I shout. "He's in Mr. Solomon's room—" A blast of foam silences me and I go down again, still encircled by the tuba. Now my arms are pinned at my sides, and I can barely move—not that I'd be much help standing up to those two Neanderthals. And if I'm upset, I can only imagine what must be going on in Joel's mind. After everything he's been through, he comes home only to find that it's starting all over again.

Kimberly bolts past the two attackers and out the door. They make no move to stop her. Their focus is on me and mostly on Joel.

"Hey, check out all these instruments," Bear snickers, as if the band room is the last place anyone might expect to find such things. "You think if I practice hard I could become a musician like the great Joel Weber?" He delivers a solid boot to the French horn, which skitters across the floor, kicking up a spray from the melting foam that covers half the room.

"Please don't touch the instruments," Joel whimpers. "I promised Mrs. Gilbride I'd be responsible for everything."

Well, that does it. Once those two idiots see how to get a rise out of Joel, they're off to the races, throwing flutes like mini javelins and Frisbeeing cymbals all around them. They roll trumpets and trombones into the slop and send violins floating on top of it. A kettledrum is upended. Music stands are hurled in all directions. Sheet music is scattered like autumn leaves.

Still stuck in the tuba, I try to scramble toward Aaron and Bear. I slip on wet paper and hit the floor with another clang. Joel has Aaron by the shoulder and is trying to pull him away from the instruments, but Aaron laughs and shakes him off.

Suddenly, Chase barrels into the room, Kimberly hot on his heels.

"What's going on?" he bellows.

"Dude, what took you so long?" Aaron crows in unholy glee. "We had to send the chick to get you!"

"This is your best idea yet," adds Bear. He hefts his fire extinguisher and hands it to Chase. "It's all yours, maestro!"

Chase looks totally blown away. I can't read his expression—shocked? Or something else?

"It's your plan," Aaron reminds him. "Bring it home!"

Chase is a statue, eyes wide.

Bear gets impatient. "Okay, I'll do it for you." He tries to take back the extinguisher, but Chase tightens his grip and holds on.

There's a vicious tug-of-war for the extinguisher. With a mighty yank, Chase wrenches it out of Bear's grasp. It swings free—just as Joel rises from the floor where Aaron tossed him.

With a thud, the heavy metal strikes Joel in the side of the face and he drops back down into the foam.

Agitated voices sound out in the hallway. Six teachers burst into the music room, Mrs. Gilbride in the lead.

"What's going on here?" she yells, taking in the wreckage all around her. *"Where's Joel Weber?"*

With a groan, Joel sits up. The foam on his face can't

disguise the fact that his left eye is already turning black-and-blue.

That's when it hits me how this must seem to the teachers. The music room is a disaster area. Instruments, music stands, books, and papers are strewn everywhere, the whole place buried in foam. The school's three most notorious bullies are right there. One of them—Chase—still wields a fire extinguisher. And their number one target—Joel—is down on the floor with a rapidly swelling face, obviously the victim of an assault.

"It isn't what it looks like!" I gasp, and then bite my tongue. What if it's *exactly* what it looks like? The idea to send for Chase came from Aaron and Bear. Was that the plan all along? And was Chase the ringleader, just like those guys said?

The teachers don't pay any attention to me. Their job is defusing the crisis. Mrs. Gilbride rushes Joel to see the nurse, and the other staff members march Aaron, Bear, and Chase off to the principal's office. Kimberly follows. Even now, her only concern is Chase.

As quickly as that, I'm all alone, still trapped in the marching band's tuba. With a heavy sigh, I struggle up and try to shake myself out of the brass tentacles of this thing. It moves maybe an inch. I'm going to be here all night.

As I continue to wriggle and squirm, dripping gray frothy shoe polish into the foam, I reflect that the worst part of this isn't being stuck in a tuba. It isn't that *One Man Band* is never going to happen. It's the sad fact that Kimberly could leave me in such a terrible state just because Chase is in trouble.

And as soon as I think that, I realize that the real worm

around here has to be me—wormier, even, than Aaron and Bear. I care more about my love life than the fact that my friend Chase might not be my friend after all.

It isn't true! I scold myself. *Chase used to be like that, but not anymore!*

Then there's the evidence of my own eyes and ears: the trashed band room. Another attack on poor Joel. Chase, right alongside his old wrecking crew, delivering the final blow.

I sit down on the edge of the riser and hang my head, too depressed to wriggle anymore.

The sound of wet sneakers squishing in the slop jolts me out of my melancholy. I look up to see Kimberly standing over me.

She says, "I thought you might need some help getting out of that thing."

My heart soars.

Hope.

CHAPTER TWENTY-ONE

CHASE AMBROSE

It should be familiar to me—sitting on the chairs outside Dr. Fitzwallace's office with Aaron and Bear, waiting for the ax to fall. Aaron assures me that our butt-prints are permanently etched into the seats. I don't remember any of that, but it's accepted fact that the three of us have spent a lot of time here.

Aaron settles himself comfortably and grins at me. "There's no place like home."

I'm not in the mood to grin back. "Are you both crazy? What was all that supposed to be about?"

Bear rolls his eyes. "Oh, boo hoo. The poor Geek Squad."

I'm furious. "Forget them—what about *me*? You've just gotten me in a ton of trouble! What about *yourselves*? You're both going to get kicked off the football team for this! And for what? So you could spray fire extinguisher foam on a bunch of band instruments?"

Bear keeps on smiling. "At least we weren't the ones who conked Joel Weber."

"That was an *accident*!"

"You think Fitzwallace is going to believe that?" Bear retorts. "Who's going to back you up? Your video dweebs? I kind of doubt you're their favorite person right now."

I'm so upset I can barely come up with the right words. "You did this on purpose to frame me! We're supposed to be friends! And you were so dead set on wrecking my life that you didn't even care if you went down the drain with me!"

Aaron's calm. "No one's going down the drain."

"Are you delusional or just stupid? With our reputation? They're going to throw the kitchen sink at us! Community service is something we can only dream about now! We're going to get *expelled*! And we'd better pray Fitzwallace isn't on the phone with the cops right now!"

"Relax," says Aaron in an undertone. "First off, we *are* friends. And we're not going to let anything bad happen to you. Just stick with us, agree with everything I say, and we've got this."

"You *are* delusional," I hiss. "How could there be any way to explain that train wreck in the music room?"

When the door to the inner office opens, the knob makes a snap like a gunshot. Then Dr. Fitzwallace is upon us, his rage all the more terrible because it's ice-cold. Honestly, I can't say I blame him. I'm not thrilled about being in trouble. But if any situation ever justified a principal losing it on three students, it's this one.

He ushers us inside and seats himself while we stand in front of his desk. "Well, it's the three of you again. I was hoping—" He looks at me and shakes his head sadly. "All right, let's hear it."

Knowing full well it's not going to get me anywhere, I'm about to protest my innocence when Aaron speaks up.

"I know it looks bad, but we didn't do anything wrong.

Bear and I were walking past the band room and saw smoke coming out from under the door. So we grabbed fire extinguishers and ran inside, spraying. They were shooting some kind of video, and they had a million lights plugged in. Something must have shorted out and caused a fire. Chase heard the yelling and came in to help us. But the video kids attacked us because their project was getting ruined. And somehow Joel Weber hit his head on one of the extinguishers."

The principal frowns. "That's not how the students on the scene described it."

Bear shakes his head understandingly. "Don't be too hard on them, Dr. Fitzwallace. They were probably just scared of getting in trouble for starting the fire."

The frown deepens. "None of my teachers smelled smoke."

Aaron sighs with relief. "Good. We got it in time."

Dr. Fitzwallace shifts his gaze from the two of them to me. "And that's what happened?"

This is it—time for me to shoot down Aaron's ridiculous lie and speak up for my own innocence. Sure, Dr. Fitzwallace will never believe I was framed. But at least I'll have the satisfaction of throwing those two guys under the bus, even if I have to go with them.

"Well?" the principal prompts.

To my astonishment, the anger is completely gone from his expression. He's waiting for my answer—and I think I know what he's hoping to hear. He's rooting for me to go along with Aaron and Bear.

Why would a principal want to let three delinquents like us off the hook after such a huge incident? I take an educated guess. It's probably a major hassle to come down hard on students the way he'd have to throw the book at Aaron, Bear, and me. Three sets of unhappy parents. Triple the paperwork. School board meetings, maybe court cases—everything in triplicate.

And—my eyes find the photographs on the wall. The two state championship pictures, my dad and me. Losing Aaron and Bear would be a blow to the Hurricanes, and it would definitely shut down any possibility of me coming back.

So I mumble, "Yeah."

"Excuse me?"

It should be an easy thing to say, but each word sits on my tongue like poison. "Yeah, what Aaron said is the way it happened."

Fitzwallace looks almost relieved, and I know I've picked the right answer. Aaron and Bear are both smiling, although they're working hard to keep the celebration inside. They've gotten away with it, and so have I.

We're not totally off the hook. We get a bit of a lecture on how we should have called for help or pulled the fire alarm before taking matters into our own hands. He tells us we need to be less impulsive and not so rough with our fellow students. Also, we're not allowed to leave on our own. He calls our parents, and they have to pick us up.

As we stand in the foyer, waiting for our rides, Aaron and Bear are raving about our "amazing escape."

"Seriously, man," Bear tells Aaron, "I've seen tap dancing before but that was *filth*! Like art."

Aaron nods. "I was afraid Chase was going to mess it up at the end, but our boy came through. Didn't I tell you he'd have our back?"

I don't say anything, but inside I'm thinking, *It's true. I covered for them. I saw a way to save my own butt and I took it.*

And in the process, I wrapped myself in their phony story and got drawn back into the old life. So this is what it was like. Make trouble. Lie. Repeat.

Luckily, those guys are so busy congratulating themselves that they don't notice I'm not adding much to the conversation.

Bear gets picked up first, then Aaron. I'm just reflecting that Mom's not going to be thrilled about having to leave work early and come get me over this when the Ambrose Electric truck rattles along the drive.

Not Mom. Dad.

He's beaming at me like I'm here to present him with a big check from the state lottery.

I climb into the passenger seat. "What?"

He reaches over and playfully punches my shoulder. "Fitzwallace told me everything, and I read between the lines. Way to go, Champ."

"It wasn't great, Dad."

He laughs. "You think that's the first time I've ever gotten a call like that about you, Aaron, and Bear? It's never great. But you got away with it. *That's* pretty great."

I almost say, "Not really." But that wouldn't be true. I could easily be buried under a mudslide of pain right now, and I'm not. I can't regret that.

What I regret is the way I got so free and clear.

When I arrive at school the next morning, Ms. DeLeo is waiting for me at my locker.

"You found out what happened," I conclude. "I'll apologize to Brendan, Joel, and Kimmy when I see them at video club."

She shakes her head sadly. "I'm sorry, Chase. You're not part of the club anymore."

Maybe I'm stupid, but that really catches me by surprise. "Nobody told you I didn't do anything wrong?" Suddenly, there's a bowling ball in my throat and I can't seem to clear it away.

"I spoke to the Webers on the phone last night," she tells me. "Joel's okay, but the family is pretty rattled, considering that the injury came from you."

"What about Brendan?" I press. "He knows I'm innocent."

"I had a talk with him too. He's not sure about your role, but the word *innocent* never came up." She shoots me a penetrating gaze. "And it doesn't help that you backed up the story that your two friends spun about an electrical fire."

My heart sinks. She's right about that. I signed on to the lie to save my own skin, but I never thought about how that would look to the video club kids. They know there was no fire.

They've all been waiting for the old me to show up. And I delivered.

"So they kicked me out," I say.

She shakes her head. "That decision was mine. I'm really sorry, Chase. You were doing so well. *Warrior* is the best middle school project I've ever seen."

I think of Shoshanna. I can only imagine how mad she must be.

"Don't worry, Ms. DeLeo," I say, surprised at how hard it is to keep my voice steady. "I'll stay away."

It bugs me, but what really bugs me is how *much* it bugs me. What do I care that a bunch of video dweebs don't want me in their club?

I bring myself up short. *Video dweebs*—that's what Aaron and Bear call them. As upset as I am, I'm not going to stoop low enough to use their words. I blame myself for the mess I'm in, but mostly I blame those two.

Speaking of Aaron and Bear, they're acting like everything is beyond awesome between us. Funny—I found a way to give them a pass for a lot of rotten stuff, including maybe even stealing a war hero's medal. But what I can't forgive them for turns out to be something I did all by myself. I protected them because it was the way to protect myself.

The cost turned out to be one video club. Plus the way I feel every time Aaron or Bear refers to me as "our boy."

I start taking weird detours through the halls just to avoid running into them.

My one consolation is this is a short day for me. Dad's

picking me up at eleven and taking me to my appointment with Dr. Nguyen, the sports medicine specialist. At least that spares me lunch at the football table. I won't be eating with the video crowd anytime soon.

Is it possible to lose your appetite for an entire school year?

I spot Brendan a couple of times, but when he sees me, he quickly turns away. I catch a glimpse of Shoshanna, scorching me with a look that would melt titanium.

I don't think Joel's even at school.

Dr. Nguyen reenters the exam room and beams at me. "Well, young man, I've got good news and better news. The good news is you exhibit no lingering concussion symptoms, and you're fit as a fiddle in every way. The better news is I'm signing the medical form authorizing you to return to the football team with no restrictions. Congratulations."

Gee, what a surprise. Dad searched and searched and found a doctor who would clear a dead man to go out there and get tackled. And only sixty miles away.

As we drive home in "the 'Stang," Dad rails against "brain-dead Cooperman," who kept me off the gridiron for no real reason.

"Dr. Cooperman has a diploma from Harvard Medical School in his office," I tell him. "I didn't see a diploma on Dr. Nguyen's wall."

Dad snorts into the wheel. "Just because he isn't one of

those Ivy League snobs doesn't mean he isn't as legit as they come. This is great news, Champ! You're back on the team!" His brow darkens. "And maybe those stumblebums will start winning again once you're out there."

"In three weeks," I remind him. "School rules. One week of non-contact practice, then two weeks in full pads before I can play in a real game."

"Just in time for a late-season playoff run," Dad chortles.

I'm not that happy about my triumphant return to football, and it isn't only because of Dr. Nguyen, who would have signed a paper certifying I was pregnant with triplets if my father had paid him enough. It's not the medical part that bothers me—I know I'm fine. Dr. Cooperman pretty much said so himself.

I'm even interested in the game and excited to see if I can be as good as everybody says I used to be.

The part I don't like is that football me is the old me, and I don't want to be that guy anymore. Look how fast my pre-amnesia instincts kicked in the minute Aaron and Bear jammed me up yesterday.

But really, what choice do I have except the Hurricanes? I'm kicked out of video club, and I lost every one of the friends I made there.

"Things are finally turning around for you, Champ," my father goes on.

"But maybe not the way I want them to," I complain.

"Why? Because a bunch of sissies are ticked off at you?"

He doesn't understand why the video club thing hurts so much. I'm not sure I understand it myself.

"It isn't just the kids. Ms. DeLeo was the one who kicked me out."

"Teachers," Dad snorts. "They have to slap you on the wrist to make it look like they're in charge. You'll notice you're not banned from the football team and neither are your buddies Aaron and Bear. When I played, I had the whole faculty wrapped around my little finger. Sure, they threw me a detention every now and then to make it look good. But after the state championship, I called the shots in that school."

For the first time, I say it out loud. "Aaron and Bear might not be my buddies anymore."

"Aw, come on, Champ, don't be that way." He beams at me. "First that mess with the Weber kid, then the accident—it feels like it took forever to get the old Chase back. Don't tell your mother, but I'm proud of the way you handled Joel. You made your statement, that's for sure."

I don't bother to point out that I wasn't making a statement with Joel. It looks more like my buddies Aaron and Bear were making a statement with me. And all it took was a sick imagination and a lot of fire extinguisher foam.

By the time we get back to Hiawassee, it's two thirty—no sense bothering to go to school. Dad drops me off at home, making me promise to report to football practice with my newly signed medical form promptly at four. And I will—not because I want to, but because I'm too depressed to resist. Unhappiness sucks all the energy out of a guy.

Upstairs in my room, I gaze out the window at the shingles of the sloping roof. For a weird instant, I actually remember sitting out there when I wanted to be alone with my thoughts. Or maybe it's not a memory at all, but something I'm imagining because I've been told so many times that's what I used to do.

On a wild impulse, I raise the window and swing a leg over the sash. Carefully—really carefully—I crawl out there. I'm expecting to be terrified after what happened. Actually, though, I'm pretty comfortable on the gently sloping shingles. It even feels familiar. It's not a flashback exactly—still, it has to come from my lost past. I definitely haven't been here lately. I swore to Mom that I'd never go out on the roof again.

But she's at work now, and never is a long time.

To my amazement, my body arranges itself into the position I'm told I used to prefer—butt planted, knees bent, feet flat on the shingles. It's a different kind of memory—muscle memory. Amnesia can't touch it.

I understand why I liked it up here. It's peaceful and private. The town is all around, but I'm above it, so nothing can reach me.

I see the school, and the football field I'll be on in a couple of hours. Not far away, toward downtown, is the Portland Street Residence, where Mr. Solway lives. And there's the park where we filmed *Leaf Man*. Just the thought of it brings the bowling ball back to my throat. That's the last time I'm ever going to get to work on one of Brendan's crazy videos.

Dad says the old Chase is back. I wanted that once. But right now the new Chase is the life I'd rather have.

And I've lost that too.

CHAPTER TWENTY-TWO

SHOSHANNA WEBER

I must be the stupidest person in the history of the world.

I get straight As in school, but obviously that doesn't mean anything. All it proves is I know how to study for a geography test. As a judge of character, I'm an F-minus.

I let that jerk, that Alpha Rat, dupe me into believing he was different, that he was a nice guy. Well, a leopard never changes his spots—and that goes double for a scheming lowlife like Chase Ambrose. Falling off a roof, having amnesia—big deal. It doesn't mean you're not a rotten person today just because you can't remember being one yesterday.

I can't even face my poor brother—and not just because his eye looks like it sustained a direct hit from a cannonball. It's all my fault. I'm the one who told my parents that the coast was clear and it was safe for Joel to come home. And I ended up bringing him back into the same line of fire that almost broke his spirit last year. I could kick myself—except for the fact that my toes are pointing in the wrong direction. I can't get anything right!

It isn't just that Chase has gone back to his bullying ways. It's that first he convinced everybody he was a new person. And we went for it, hook, line, and sinker—not just me, but the video club, the teachers, Dr. Fitzwallace, the whole school. That must have been his plan all along—to lull us into a false sense of security before pouncing one more time. What a plan it was—to ruin Brendan's video, wreck the music room, attack Joel, and blame the whole thing on an imaginary fire. Chase was behind it from the very beginning. From a strategy standpoint, you almost have to admire it. It sure succeeded with flying colors. And Joel has the colors to prove it—black-and-blue, mostly.

I wish I could take my video project and flush it down the toilet. I'd rather lose all that time and throw away the best work I've ever done than have anything linking my name to Chase Ambrose. Compared to what's happened to my brother, the National Video Journalism Contest is about as meaningful as counting snowflakes in a blizzard. That's another reason to hate myself—that I would let my ambition to win a lousy contest make me so blind. I never should have allowed myself to be pushed into partnering up with Chase no matter what Brendan and Ms. DeLeo said. I don't care that the project is on a really great and interesting guy. It wouldn't make any difference if we got an interview with all the signers of the Declaration of Independence, brought back to life and re-formed into a boy band. It just isn't worth it.

For the smartest kid in school, Brendan's even dumber than I am. He's got it in his thick head that there's a chance Chase might be innocent.

"I don't know, Shoshanna," he insists. "It was Aaron and

Bear who busted up the shoot. Chase could have been trying to stop them."

"Oh, sure," I return. "And he just happened to show up at exactly the right moment."

"He didn't 'show up,'" he argues. "I sent Kimberly to get him."

"Joel said *you* didn't send her for Chase; *they* did."

"There was a lot going on," he admits. "It's hard to remember. I think they sent her first, and then I did."

"Why couldn't you go yourself?"

"Because I was stuck in the tuba," he replies, as if it's the most natural thing in the world. Happens to everyone, right?

"Listen," I tell him. "My poor brother has a Technicolor face, courtesy of the guy you say 'might' be innocent."

"That could have been an accident—a tug-of-war with the fire extinguisher. Maybe Chase was trying to *protect* Joel."

I roll my eyes. "Let him protect somebody else. When it came time to lie his way out of the blame, he was right there with Aaron and Bear. That's all the proof I need."

"I know what it looks like," he agrees reluctantly. "But doesn't Chase deserve the benefit of the doubt?"

"Listen," I challenge. "If what you say is true, then Aaron and Bear set him up and nearly got him kicked out of school. And where is he this very minute? At football practice with the same Aaron and Bear, who should be his worst enemies. What does that tell you?"

"Well, it's not like he can come to video club anymore—"

"And in the cafeteria," I persist, "who does he eat lunch with? The football team."

"We won't let him at our table."

"We're protecting Joel. That's the *real* meaning of protection—not cold-cocking someone with a fire extinguisher. I'm so mad at that jerk, and you should be too. He's like a cobra. He lured us in until we trusted him. Then he struck. And now he's slithered back to his old life as if nothing ever happened. Joel may be the one who's bleeding, but the attack was on all of us."

And he agrees. Brendan knows I'm right, however much he wants to convince himself that Chase is innocent. The whole club knows that we're better off without a guy like that.

So how come his name keeps popping up again and again at our meetings?

"That camera work looks a little shaky. You've got to keep it smooth, like Chase . . ."

"Yeah, that's a cool shot. It was Chase's idea to film it worm's-eye view . . ."

"The kid's a mumbler, but you can hear the audio clearly because Chase lay on the floor and held the microphone just out of frame . . ."

"Can we please stop talking about Chase Ambrose?" I explode. "He's not a god—he's just a person, and a *lousy* person at that! He *belongs* on the football team with the other muscleheads. Actually, he belongs chained to a slab of concrete at the bottom of the Marianas Trench, but I'll take the football team if it gets him away from us."

Joel has been silent throughout all this. Now he speaks up.

"Am I the only one who's noticed that video club has gotten kind of lousy?"

"What are you saying?" I demand.

He shrugs. "We all watched *Warrior*. It's fantastic. Nobody's doing that kind of work anymore—"

I'm furious. "You think that's because we don't have *him*?"

My brother looks at me with his one good eye. "Just because I hate Chase Ambrose doesn't mean I fall to pieces every time someone mentions his name. Go ahead. Talk about him. I can handle it. This isn't last year. No matter what, I'm not going to be 'chased' out of town again."

We slap him on the back and pound his shoulder. A few of us even cheer. It almost reminds me of the football team, although I'd never admit it. Ms. DeLeo gives him a big hug.

Maybe I can stop beating myself up for getting Mom and Dad to bring him home from Melton. The very worst happened and he's okay.

I look at my "little" brother, fourteen minutes younger than me.

He's growing up.

CHAPTER TWENTY-THREE

CHASE AMBROSE

At football practice, when everybody else is laboring under a ton of equipment, and you're breezing through the drills in shorts and a T-shirt, you're not the most popular guy on the field. All around me, the gridiron resounds with crunching tackles, *oofs*, and grunts of pain, but I'm immune to that. No contact for the first week of my comeback—middle school rules.

My teammates manage to see to it that I suffer just the same. Around the Gatorade bucket, no drink in my hand makes it as far as my mouth. It's pretty clear the other players have determined that I'm not going to get so much as a sip as long as my special treatment holds up. Every time I've got a full cup, someone manages to jostle my elbow until the contents spill down my leg and into my cleats. It's been going on for three days now. I'm borderline dehydrated, and when I walk, my wet pants create squishing noises.

"Hey, Pink!" Coach Davenport calls, referring to the fruit punch color of my lower body. "Get out there and catch some passes!"

I have no memory of what practice is supposed to be like. But I don't complain about the treatment, and focus on doing my job. I guess playing football is like riding a bicycle. You never really forget how. I run hard, and after a couple of days, the cuts and jukes come back to me—more muscle memory. I make a few good grabs, and I can feel the guys' attitudes thawing a little.

"Nice catch, captain," Landon tells me with a slap where my shoulder pad would be if I was wearing one.

I guess I'm still the captain. I didn't forfeit that by having amnesia.

"Yeah, good to have you back," adds Joey in a tone that could almost be interpreted as friendly.

I try to turn this development to my advantage. "Can I have a drink now?"

He laughs. "Bathroom's in the field house, newbie."

I hadn't thought of that. Pretty soon I'm in there, bent over the sink, guzzling water from the tap. It's better than drinking out of the toilet, which is probably what Joey had in mind.

It takes a while, but Landon finally explains that this is standard procedure for anyone who's on non-contact. As soon as I'm getting tackled like everybody else, my Gatorade privileges will be restored.

Football.

Here's a surprise: I like it. That means everything didn't change when I fell on my head. It proves that you can be an athlete and a video club kid at the same time. Not in my case, obviously. Video club invited me to get lost. But it's *possible* to be both. I have no idea why more people don't do it. Maybe it's because the jocks will never find out if they enjoy doing something artsy because they'll never try it. And the arts kids feel the same way about sports.

In spite of everything that's happened, I'm getting the hang of most of the Hurricanes. They're a rowdy crew, and sometimes the physical nature of the game spills over into the way they treat other kids—which is definitely not right. But they're giving me a chance, which is more than I can say for video club these days. I'm starting to see how I could have been friends with the players.

With two exceptions.

Aaron and Bear finally have what they wanted: My name is mud with my new friends and I'm back on the team. But if they expect us to be the Three Musketeers again, they can forget it. They couldn't stand to see me making a life for myself that didn't include them, so they wrecked it for me—and in the process, they managed to retarget poor Joel, who hasn't even been home for two weeks yet. And that's not including the way they treat the residents at Portland Street. But the last straw was when they cornered me so I had no choice but to lie to Dr. Fitzwallace to protect the three of us. Aaron's always lecturing me about friendship. He doesn't know the meaning of the word.

I don't talk to them. I don't stretch next to them. In the locker room, I sit so far away from them that I'm practically out in the hall. When we're on the practice field for the same drill, they get no chatter from me. Not even any eye contact.

The other Hurricanes have started to notice, but they think it's funny. Aaron and Bear don't. And how much do I care about hurting their delicate feelings? Well, you could fit that inside the nucleus of a carbon atom.

On Friday, Coach Davenport runs us through a quick workout. The Hurricanes have a night game tomorrow, and he wants everybody fresh but sharp. Since I won't be playing, he keeps me out on the field while the others clatter into the locker room.

"Ten laps, Pink," he calls. "No dogging it."

The others are laughing at me and calling out mock encouragement—their revenge for my week of no pads. To show off, I kick into high gear and sprint down the sideline. One thing that's come out of this first week of practice—I've gotten really fast. None of my teammates are very impressed, because, apparently, I was always this fast. But it's news to me—and these days, I need something to make me feel good about myself.

When the tackle comes, it's a complete shock. One second I'm running free and the next, a big body hits me just below the knees, knocking my legs out from under me and sending me hurtling forward. I must somersault, because I see a quick panorama of sky and grass. The earth comes up to clobber me. I think I eat some of it.

Gasping, I roll over. A helmeted figure is blocking out the sun. Number 57—Bear. Aaron stands beside him, applauding.

"How's that for non-contact?" Bear spits.

I don't answer. I can't. The wind is totally knocked out of me. I just lie there, wheezing.

"Oops," he goes on, fake apologetic. "I think that might have been contact. It's so confusing with you lately, Ambrose.

You're a friend; you're an enemy. You're a teammate; you're a video dork. You've got amnesia"—he grabs me by the fabric of my T-shirt and hauls me to my feet—"or maybe you remember more than you let on!"

"I've got no pads on!" I choke, finding breath at last. "You want to kill me? It could happen, you know! And you'd get more than community service for that!"

"We had to get your attention, man," Aaron informs me solemnly. "You've barely said a word to us all week."

"Don't worry, we won't harm a hair on your little head," Bear adds. "Not until we get square."

"Get *square*?" I don't know if I've ever been so mad. "Aren't we square yet? All my friends hate my guts because they think I set up what happened in the band room!"

Aaron grins. "It wasn't too hard to convince them either. I guess we're not the only ones who figured out that the 'new' Chase is a phony."

"What are you talking about?" I sputter.

"You never had any amnesia!" Bear accuses harshly. "You faked the whole thing!"

"Are you crazy?" I demand. "What's so fantastic about forgetting your whole life that anybody would fake it? I didn't even know my own mother!"

"Well, for one thing," Bear returns readily, "you can act like you have no clue what you owe us!"

"I owe you *nothing*!" I seethe. "The fact that I used to be friends with you guys makes me sick! If you think you can push me around the way you do everybody else, think again!

There's still enough of the old Chase left to take you on. You're lucky I don't go straight to the cops and rat you out for swiping Mr. Solway's medal!"

They stare at me in surprise. I can feel the advantage shifting to me, so I don't let up. "Yeah, geniuses, I figured that out by watching you prowling the halls of Portland Street, taking advantage of the people you're supposed to be helping. Give me credit for having the brains to see who's sleazy enough to steal from a war hero who's too frail to look after his stuff!"

Bear is still staring, but slow understanding is dawning on Aaron.

"You—you really *do* have amnesia," he tells me.

"Yeah? So?"

"So you don't remember. *We* didn't jack that medal—*you* did."

Rage floods through me, and I rear back my fist to take a swing at him. Before I can act, though, the memory flashes in my brain. The triangular case on the dresser, flipped open to reveal the gleaming five-pointed Medal of Honor at the end of its blue star-spangled ribbon. A hand reaches down for it.

My hand.

I'm totally appalled, yet it makes perfect sense. Aaron and Bear are the worst people I know, but they weren't always a twosome. They had a ringleader. Chase Ambrose. And in those days, if they were low, he was lower.

Even before the memory returned, I should have known I did it.

Bear's words break into my horrified thoughts. "That's

right, Boy Scout, this one's on you. You didn't even wait till the old Dumbledore was out of the room. As soon as his back was turned, you snatched it and tossed the case in the closet. It's worth big money, and you owe us our share."

"Three-way split, that was our deal," Aaron confirms. "If we were sentenced to the Graybeard Motel, at least we were going to get something out of it."

"I—I don't have it."

Bear's brow darkens. "Don't lie, man! I saw you jam it in your pocket and walk out of the building!"

"No—" I all but whisper. "I mean, I might have it. But I don't know what I did with it. And if I do find it, it's going back to Mr. Solway. Maybe I used to be a crook, but I'm not one anymore."

Aaron steps forward. "Fine. You're better than us now. You're a saint. But when you took that medal—that was the old you and the old rules. So it belongs to all three of us. You can't do anything without our okay, and we don't give it."

He looks totally serious, like a lawyer reading a contract.

"You make a move without us, you'll regret it," Bear adds threateningly.

"I regret I ever met you guys!" I shout, hoarse with emotion. I wheel away from them and flee for home, not even stopping in the locker room to shower and change. I have to put as much distance as possible between myself and those two.

As I run, hot tears of shame are streaming down my face.

Since my accident, I've heard a lot about the person I used to be. Never did I imagine this.

I sprint harder, accelerating onto the sidewalk, outpacing even the most intense drills from practice. It's no problem escaping Aaron and Bear.

But I'll never be able to get away from myself.

CHAPTER TWENTY-FOUR

BRENDAN ESPINOZA

Kimberly's gone.

I don't mean she's dead or anything drastic like that. She hasn't even moved away. Just gone from my life.

That time in the music room when she cared enough to help me out of the tuba when I was too slick with fire extinguisher foam to get any traction, I really believed that I was starting to make some progress with her. But it turns out that was wishful thinking.

In the end, she was just hanging around to be close to Chase. Now that he's kicked out, she's stopped coming to meetings. From an artistic standpoint, that's probably a good thing.

Now she's back supporting the football team, since Chase is on it again. She even watches practice, sitting in the stands, her homework binder propped open on her lap. It makes me sad, because that's the same thing she did at video club. These days, the closest I ever get to her is when we happen to pass in the hall, and she looks like she's trying to remember where she knows me from.

You'd think all that would make me really jealous of Chase. And it does—sort of. But the truth is, I probably miss Chase even more than I miss Kimberly. Video club is useless without him. We might as well change the name to Club, because the creativity level in that room is basically zero. The others notice it too. It's pretty obvious when Ms. DeLeo asks who's got footage to screen, and nobody has squat.

Even though our club is grinding to a halt, I have no sympathy for those guys. I can't get any of them even to consider the possibility that Chase might be innocent. Or maybe they're right and I'm the moron. Chase didn't hesitate to lie about what happened in the music room and blame everything on our electrical cables. Whatever he did or didn't do to Joel and *One Man Band*, he was just as bad as his Neanderthal pals in that way.

But he was our friend. I refuse to believe he was faking that. He was a good club member—maybe the best. He worked shoulder to shoulder with Shoshanna on *Warrior*, which is the greatest thing we ever produced. She should have at least taken the time to listen to his side of the story.

If there is such a thing.

Anyway, she didn't. And neither did Hugo or Mauricia or Barton or even me. We were fine to benefit from his talent when he was with us, but we never really believed that he wasn't the Chase Ambrose we used to know. And the first time something went wrong, we dropped him like a hot potato.

The whole thing depresses me to the point where I almost want to quit video club. But I'm the president; if I leave it'll fall apart for sure. No, it's up to me to jump-start my fellow vidiots. Even though they don't deserve it, I'm going to make a video—*any* video—just to get our creative juices flowing again.

Unfortunately, I have zero ideas—that's how blocked this Chase business has made everybody. So I take a walk up and down the street, just for a change of scenery. And I see it.

There's a big, fat slug that's been climbing the stucco side of our house for the past day and a half. He's not making a heck of a lot of progress. He's only a third of the way up after all that time, which means he's averaging, by my calculations, like, fifteen feet per week. But you have to admire the little guy's spirit. He's absolutely determined to get where he's going—which is the roof, I guess. I don't know what's up there for him. That's his problem, not mine.

I decide to film his journey, inch by inch up the side, defying gravity. I'll call it *Slugfest*, or maybe something lofty and inspirational, like *The Ascent*. Then, in editing, I can add in commentary, like he's pushing for the summit of Everest, or maybe play-by-play from the Indy 500. That could be kind of funny—sportscasters raving about speed and acceleration and afterburners while he's millimetering along.

Okay, it's no *Leaf Man*. But hopefully it'll get the video club going again.

I take the flip-cam out of my backpack—I always bring one home in case inspiration strikes—and mount it on my tripod. That way, I can shoot hours of video without having to cool my heels watching nothing happening. Outside, I arrange the whole setup on our side walkway, with the camera pointing up so that Sluggo is dead center of the frame. It's not as if he's going to zoom out of the picture anytime soon—not unless someone straps a tiny booster rocket onto his butt, or whatever slugs have back there.

I press the record button and nothing happens—no pulsing green light to indicate filming. Weird. We recharge the camera batteries every day. I try again. Still nothing. That's when I notice the message flashing on the viewfinder: MEMORY FULL.

That's impossible. Club rules say you have to download your footage onto a computer or a memory stick so we can wipe the camera for the next user. Ms. DeLeo is a real tyrant about it. How did this one get missed? And if the memory's full, what's on it?

I press the play button. The first thing I hear out of the flip-cam's tiny speaker is a high-octane full-orchestra rendition of "For He's a Jolly Good Fellow." Then I see myself in a dark suit and bow tie on band risers in front of a green screen. I'm in a chair with a clarinet in my hands, pretending to play along with the fast-paced music. As I watch, transfixed, clarinet-Brendan disappears, to be replaced in a jump cut by another version of myself sitting in the same chair a few feet away. This time I've got a violin, and I'm fiddling like mad in furious time with the song. That goes on for a little while, and then, just as suddenly, I'm seated at a drum set on the highest riser, my arms just a blur.

It hits me. This is *One Man Band*! I must have started the camera, and in all the excitement, I never switched it off. Come to think of it, I never turned in the camera that afternoon. Kimberly did it for me while I was in the bathroom trying to clean up my suit, which was hemorrhaging shoe polish all over the school. And Kimberly being Kimberly, she didn't know the rule about wiping the memory. She just put the camera back on the shelf.

Amazing! I thought *One Man Band* was gone forever. And here it is on this flip-cam, ready to be cut into my greatest video ever. Obviously, I won't be able to use the tuba part, because that's when we got attacked and the whole shoot got busted up. After all, my band can't feature a tuba player who gets slimed with foam and trapped in his own instrument. But the rest of it—breathlessly, I fast-forward—it's all okay. Better than okay! This could be my first YouTube video to hit the big time!

I scan right to the end, and it's all there—Aaron and Bear raiding the shoot, Kimberly running out to get Chase, and finally the tug-of-war between him and Bear with the fire extinguisher. Even over the loud music, you can actually hear the *whack* when the heavy metal casing smashes Joel in the eye. I wince a little at that. No wonder half the poor guy's face is black-and-blue. That had to hurt. I'll bet it still does.

Also—and this is important—no smoke, no fire. No reason to fill the room with foam. Not that I ever took *that* story seriously. Still, it's nice to see hard evidence.

Evidence . . .

I'm so wrapped up in reliving it that it takes a few seconds to realize that I'm looking at something monumentally important. All that craziness in the music room happened so fast that it was impossible to process it. But here's a visual record that I can watch over and over again to catch every detail.

So I back up the clip to the moment Chase bursts onto the scene and run it in super-slo-mo. He looks shocked—if he planned this, he has to be the greatest actor in the world. When Bear hands him the fire extinguisher, he takes it, but he just stands there holding it, as if he has no idea what it is or why he has it. He never fires it or even holds it upright. It's like he's in a daze—until Bear tries to grab the thing back. Then Chase wakes up, and the struggle is on to keep it away from Bear. And when he pulls it free and it swings back and hits Joel—

Pure accident.

Maybe afterward he helped Aaron and Bear cover up what they did. But this video *proves* that Chase was trying to stop the attack, not to join in.

I'm practically bursting out of my skin with excitement. I want to run in fifteen different directions to spread the word far and wide. Who should I tell first? Chase? Ms. DeLeo? Dr. Fitzwallace? It's more than just about video club; it's about justice!

And don't forget Joel himself. He shouldn't be allowed to go on thinking that Chase still has it out for him. And Shoshanna—she's a nice person and a great vidiot, but let's face it—right now, she'd burn Chase at the stake if she thought she could get away with it. She needs to know what really happened. All the vidiots do.

I frown. It's the weekend. None of us will be at school until Monday. This has to be done right. The school can wait, but the video club should see this footage. It's more than just evidence. It'll be nothing less than a demonstration of the power of the moving image to change hearts and minds. Who better than the president of the video club to make it happen?

I take out my phone and compose a text to Chase, Shoshanna, and Joel:

> Urgent! Come to my house at 10 a.m. tomorrow. There's something important you have to see. PS: I'm not trying to rope you into helping with another YouTube video.

After some agonized soul-searching, I send the same text to Kimberly, but add a line that says:

> PS: Chase is going to be there.

Okay, I want to see her again.

Sue me.

CHAPTER TWENTY-FIVE

CHASE AMBROSE

There's something important you have to see.

I stare at Brendan's text on my phone. What's this big deal he needs to show me? Probably nothing—chances are, he really *is* just trying to rope me into helping with a new YouTube video, although he says that's not it.

I don't care. The fact that he texted me at all is something. I haven't heard a peep from any of the video club kids since that day in the music room. Who can blame them? They all heard how I lied about the electrical fire.

And they don't even know about the *really* bad thing I did.

To be honest, I'd give anything to be part of one of Brendan's goofball videos again. They're always hilarious, and I could use a good laugh right about now. I can't remember the last time I laughed. Nothing has been funny lately, and the most un-funny part is what I just found out about myself. Yeah, Aaron and Bear are jerks, my dad's pushy, and the video club has turned on me. But I'm worse than all of them. I'm a criminal, and the fact that I don't remember it doesn't change what I did.

How could I do such a thing? It's a question that doesn't need answering. *I* didn't do it; the *old* me did. And it's no mystery that the old me was capable of some pretty awful stuff. *I* stole Mr. Solway's Medal of Honor from his room at Portland Street—one sleazy act of many, courtesy of Chase, Aaron, and Bear. I have no idea what I planned to do with it. Sell it, probably, and split the money with my two accomplices. But that little plan went sour when I stashed it somewhere, and then went and got amnesia and couldn't remember my hiding place. No wonder Aaron and Bear were so suspicious of me. They thought I was holding out on them so I could keep the profit for myself. And the worst part is that I can't even give the medal back to Mr. Solway, because I have absolutely no idea what I did with it. And I don't know how to find out.

Maybe it'll come back to me in bits and pieces like some of my past. But when? It could take *years.* What if Mr. Solway dies in the meantime? How will I ever make it right?

It's funny—the idea of going back to Brendan's house stings, even though I've only been there once before. When I had the accident, I never longed for my old life because I couldn't remember it. But my *new* old life—video club and my new friends—losing *that* hurts a lot, since this time I know what I'm missing. And it hurts twice as much because of how quick those guys were to turn against me. Maybe that means we were never really friends, even though I thought we were. My partnership with Shoshanna felt that way for sure. When the two of us were working side by side, interviewing Mr. Solway and editing *Warrior*, I was positive that we were creating something amazing together. All the kids in video club were finally starting to trust me. Even Joel was kind of warming up to me. Or so I thought. I must have been nuts.

In the end, that's why I decide to go to Brendan's. If he's reaching out to me, that's a good thing.

I leave the house and step into a beehive of activity. Boxes and furniture are scattered all over the lawn next door. Four big guys are loading everything into a moving truck. That's right—the Tottenhams are moving today. Supposedly, they're really nice neighbors who were great to Johnny and me growing up. Mom is sad that they're moving. I have no clue, of course. When you've got amnesia, it's hard enough to relearn the important people in your life. You tend to lose the crowd on the fringes.

I'm cutting across the grass in the direction of Brendan's when two of the movers step out the front door carrying a large framed painting. I gasp and, for a second, forget to breathe.

It's *her*!

The little girl in the blue dress trimmed in white lace—my only memory that stuck with me through the accident! I think about the hours I spent agonizing over that image—where it came from, and whether I might have hallucinated the whole thing. But no, here she is, the same red ribbon in her blond hair. I see details that aren't in my memory—like she's standing in a garden surrounded by flowers, and there's a little watering can in her hand.

I didn't imagine her at all. I *remembered* her from the painting in my neighbors' house!

I run over to Mrs. Tottenham, who is wringing her hands over the handling of a carton marked SUPERFRAGILE!!!

"That painting!" I exclaim, my voice hoarse. "Did you ever show it to me?"

"Oh, hello, Chase." She chuckles. "That's just a reproduction, of course. An original Renoir would be worth tens of millions of dollars."

"Yeah, okay," I say breathlessly. "But why do I know it? Did I ever see it in your place?"

"I don't think so, dear," she tells me. "It was hanging in the upstairs solarium."

I follow her pointing finger to the glassed-in sunroom on the second floor of the house. So I didn't see it. But I *did*! How else could it be the only image to make the trip through my shattered memory?

My eyes travel from the Tottenham home to ours next door. Could I have looked inside their solarium from one of our upstairs windows? No way. The entrance to our house is around the corner, facing away from theirs. Our dormer is in front. That sunroom faces nothing but a chimney and some sloped shingles. The only way to see that painting from our place would be to climb to the top of our roof and peer over the peak down into the huge glass window.

And suddenly, I just know. I run back inside, tear up the stairs to my bedroom, and step out onto the perch that was so much a part of my old life. I start to climb, my rubber-soled sneakers clinging to the rough shingles. The dormer, which houses my room, is beside me. But that leaves a sloped path about three feet wide, leading straight up to the top.

As comfortable as I am on the section of roof right outside my window, the steep slog to the peak is another ballgame. The grade is sharp, and the higher I go, the clearer the image of exactly what must have happened over the summer becomes—and how far I must have fallen. The ground seems so distant it should be in another zip code. I'm amazed I didn't dash my brains out on the grass.

I get on my hands and knees, and my ascent becomes a crawl. I feel a little more secure this way, especially as I near the apex, where I can use my right arm to cling to the dormer. I'm pretty scared, but I'm even more determined to get up there. For me to remember the little girl in blue, she must have been the last thing I saw before the accident. That makes sense, since the roof is the only place I could have seen her from. I can't explain it, but I'm positive the key to what happened to me lies a few feet ahead.

I stretch out my arm, get a grip on the top of the A-frame, and haul myself up to gaze down at the Tottenhams' house. There it is, the floor-to-ceiling window of the sunroom. I can even make out the large faded rectangle on the wall where the picture must have hung.

Okay, I think, *this is where I was when I fell.* But it still doesn't answer the big question: Why did I come up here? Was I spying on the Tottenhams in their sunroom? I was rotten enough. But why would I care what they were doing? Besides, according to Mom, we were friends. I could have just knocked on their door. Why bother to climb halfway to the moon?

Frustration wells up in me, mingling with my disappointment. So the little girl in the blue dress tells me where I fell from, but that's it.

As I inch my way back from the peak, I extend my right arm, steadying myself against the cedar shakes on the side of the dormer. No sense repeating my swan dive off the roof, although it's no more than I deserve. I almost slip as one of the shakes pulls away. A terrified gasp escapes me as I slide a little before stopping my descent with my feet. I hang on like a fly to a wall, while the racing of my pulse returns to normal.

That's when I catch a glimpse of blue behind the dull brown of the loose shake. There's something back there, wedged in behind the loose wood. I know what it is even before I reach for it.

My hand closes on the silky blue ribbon, and as I draw it out, I feel the weight of the military decoration attached to it. The gold five-pointed star catches briefly on some insulation. And there it is, Mr. Solway's Medal of Honor—stolen, hidden, forgotten, and discovered again.

Then, as if finding the medal has unclogged a drain, the memory of my accident pours back into me. It starts at the apex of the roof, with me gloating over the brilliance of my hiding place, while peering down through the sunroom window at Mr. Tottenham next door. He's in the lotus position on the floor, performing awkward yoga in front of the painting of the girl in blue. That's what does me in—the hilarious sight of my overweight neighbor twisted into a pretzel, looking like a giant mutant lemon in his skintight fluorescent yellow workout suit.

I let go for just a second, reaching for my phone to get a picture of this one-man comedy routine. And the next thing I know, I'm skidding down the roof, the rectangular pattern of the shingles becoming a blur as I pick up speed.

I claw madly at the slope, desperate for a handhold, a foothold—anything to stop my descent. It's no use. My momentum is too much. I'm falling.

When I hit the eaves I flip over a little, giving me a terrifying view of the yard as it screams up to meet me. I know dizzying acceleration, and—

I brace for impact, but the memory ends there. I don't have to hit the ground a second time.

So that's how it happened—the mishap that turned my entire life upside down and almost killed me. Serves me right for snooping on poor Mr. Tottenham. How is it my business if he wants to do yoga in form-fitting spandex? But that was the old Chase. *Everything* was his business, because he said it was.

What was I planning to do with that picture if I'd managed to get the phone out of my pocket? Show Aaron and Bear and the football team? Post it on Facebook? Print up fifty copies and plaster them all over town?

I sigh. Who knows why that Chase did what he did? I should probably just be grateful I don't have to be him anymore.

The medal clutched tightly in my palm, I climb down gingerly, careful to keep both hands and feet on the roof at all times. My mind is whirling. Brendan's house will just have to wait. Nothing there can be as important as returning this to its rightful owner. I have to see Mr. Solway.

Near the eaves, I slide on my butt to my window and throw a leg over the sill.

"Chase?"

Uh-oh. Mom.

"You promised you wouldn't go out on the roof ever again. Do I have to nail your window shut—?"

I just blow past her. "Sorry, Mom," I toss over my shoulder. "Gotta get to Portland Street."

"I'm not finished yelling at you yet! Have you forgotten what happened to you last summer? Do you have amnesia about the amnesia?"

I run down the stairs, calling, "I'll explain later." In the kitchen, I snatch a soft dish towel off the drying rack and wrap it around the medal. I jam it in my pocket and blast out the door.

CHAPTER TWENTY-SIX

JOEL WEBER

My black eye doesn't hurt anymore, although I look like I lost a game of chicken with an Amtrak train.

Appearance-wise, the healing process might be worse than the bruise itself. It's when the swelling starts to go down that the new colors sprout up amid the black-and-blue. Purples, greens, yellows. Every time I catch my reflection, there's a whole different palette in the piece of modern art on my face. I saw a little bit of orange yesterday.

I'm the only one in my family who finds the changing colors around my eye socket so intriguing. In a weird way, it's easier on me. If I'm sick of looking at myself, all I have to do is stay away from mirrors. My parents don't have that option. When they see my black eye—in any of its stages of evolution—they're stricken with guilt.

"Maybe it was the wrong decision to bring you home," my father reflects sadly.

"Of course it wasn't wrong," I try to assure them. "I hated Melton."

"But aren't you afraid that"—my mother lets out a short wheezing sob in C sharp—"*it* might be starting up again?"

Afraid? Sure I am. When Chase, Aaron, and Bear were all

over me last year, it was painful, humiliating, and downright scary. If you can't even ride your bike without a lacrosse stick sailing out of nowhere and sending you flying, life becomes impossible. You know it's not your fault; you know those guys are idiots. And yet you can't help thinking you somehow deserve it; that you might be just a teeny bit less *worthy* than everybody else. After all, how come no one is picking on any of them?

But as worried as I am about all that, I think what bothers me the most is how wrong I was about Chase. I honestly believed he'd changed. I was even starting to like the guy. It goes to show how mistaken a person can be.

My parents' reaction is bad enough. My *sister's* is off the chain. Every change in the bruise topography of my face launches her into a new revenge fantasy about what she would do to Chase "if I were in charge of the world." Some of these are so brutal and, in some cases, so downright gross, that I have to cut her off.

"Come on, Shosh!" I exclaim as the two of us head for Brendan's house on Sunday morning. "Listen to yourself. Like you'd ever put another human being through a wood chipper!"

"I never said another human being," she replies evenly. "I said Alpha Rat. And if you were paying attention, I said I'd feed him in feetfirst. That way, he gets to watch while his whole lower body—"

"Enough!" I interrupt. "You wouldn't do that. Nobody would do that. The Spanish Inquisition didn't do that."

"Only because the wood chipper hadn't been invented yet," she tells me sullenly.

"Anyway," I sigh, anxious to change the subject. "I wonder what Brendan wants."

"What do you think?" she snarls, still in a bad mood. "He has another stupid idea for a YouTube video, and we're the cast and crew."

"The text said that's not it," I remind her.

"It better not be. Otherwise, *Brendan's* going in the wood chipper."

That's my sister. No problem's ever so small that she can't overreact to it.

We start up the Espinozas' front walk and come face-to-face with Kimberly.

"Oh, hi, guys." She gives me a long, hard look. "Your eye is—better," she adds dubiously.

"I'm okay," I say quickly. I don't want Shosh to nominate any more candidates for the wood chipper.

"You also got the text?" my sister asks Kimberly.

She nods. "And Chase is coming too."

What? Chase?

Shosh grabs my arm and starts dragging me back down the walk.

Brendan explodes out the front door and runs up to us. "Where are you going?"

"Chase Ambrose isn't coming anywhere near me or my brother!" Shosh seethes.

"That's why I invited you! Chase is innocent!"

She keeps pulling me along.

"Well, not totally innocent," Brendan pleads. "But he didn't hit Joel on purpose! He was just as blindsided as we were! I've got proof!"

"What proof?" I ask.

"One Man Band," he explains. "The video survived. And it proves that Chase was trying to stop Aaron and Bear."

"We're going home," Shosh insists.

"*You* go home," I tell her. "I'm staying."

"Here?" she demands. "With that guy coming over?"

This time, I don't let her push me around. "I want to know what happened. I have to see it for myself."

And she stays too, probably because she thinks I need protection. A lot of guys would be embarrassed about that, but I'm at least a little bit grateful. At any minute, Chase is going to walk in Brendan's front door, and I can't predict how I'm going to feel about it. I've seen him around school here and there. Still, this will be the first time since the fire extinguisher incident that we'll be in the same room together.

We establish ourselves on the living room couch and Brendan sets up his computer on the coffee table. "I transferred this from one of the flip-cams," he explains. "I brought it home to shoot something else and this was on it."

He puts out some snacks, and we settle in to wait for Chase. Twenty minutes go by. Then we're up to half an hour.

Kimberly is impatient, mostly because Chase is the only reason she's here. "Where is he?"

Brendan texts again. No answer.

"Well, what did you expect?" Shosh scoffs.

"He said he was coming," Brendan insists.

"He cares as much about you as he cares about everybody else except himself—zero. Face it—he blew you off." My sister stands up. "Let's go, Joel. We've already wasted enough of our lives, courtesy of Chase Ambrose."

I turn to Brendan. "Play the video. Chase can see it some other time."

We fast-forward through most of it, watching musician Brendan popping up all around the risers, playing different instruments for his "one man band." He switches into regular playback once the tuba sequence comes up. I feel my stomach muscles tense. As much as I've been bullied, I've never had the opportunity to actually watch it happen before.

The impatient expression on Shosh's face is replaced by one of intense concentration.

"I don't get it," Kimberly puts in. "All I see is Brendan. Where's everybody else?"

"You and Joel are there, but you're both out of frame," Brendan explains. "Keep watching."

We hear Aaron and Bear fling the doors open, even though they're off camera. The first thing we actually see are two jets of white foam that catch Brendan full in the face. He goes down, tuba and all. It would be funny if I didn't know what was coming next. When the streams of foam change direction to some target offscreen to the right, I know I'm the one in the line of fire. There's a lot of yelling going on, and I hear my own voice in there with Brendan, Kimberly, and the two attackers.

After a few more blasts of foam, Aaron and Bear step into the frame, appearing on the left side of the screen. The next part I remember all too well. Aaron and Bear are tossing instruments all over the place and trashing the band room. I try to take on Aaron, but he shoves me down into the foam.

It's hard to watch, but not as hard as I thought it would be. *This is not who I am*, I tell myself. *It's just something that happened to me.* Somehow, seeing it unfold in real time, in high-definition video, I'm able to expand the fracas in the band room to include every rotten bullying thing that was ever done to me. And here I am, alive, undamaged—well, except my eye.

I've been victimized, but I don't have to let that define me as a victim.

I'm back—back at home and back to myself.

That's when Chase makes his appearance on the computer screen. He seems totally stunned by what he finds, even when Bear thrusts the fire extinguisher into his arms. I sit forward eagerly, because that's *my* fire extinguisher—the one that's about to bash me in the eye. As I watch Chase and Bear struggling over the shiny metal cylinder, I tense, knowing it's coming any second. I'm following the combatants, checking for the high sign, the nod of acknowledgment that shows that the three are in cahoots, and it's time to clobber the kid who got them put on community service.

It doesn't come. Chase wins the tug-of-war, and my face gets in the way. That's all that happens.

Brendan pauses the video. "An accident," he says triumphantly.

"I agree," I tell him.

"Wow, Chase must be really strong," is what Kimberly gets out of it.

Shosh's cheeks are bright red as she digests the truth. My sister judges everything and everybody so harshly that when her judgment falls on herself, it's like the end of the world.

"He still lied," she says, tight-lipped.

"He's not perfect," Brendan agrees. "But think of the trouble he would have been facing if he'd gotten blamed for all that. If it was you, and you saw an easy way out, wouldn't you take it?"

Shosh is stubborn. "I wouldn't *be* in a mess like that, because I don't hang around with pond scum!"

I look at her. "We have to at least talk to him."

I'm expecting more of an argument. But she nods. "And I can think of plenty of things to say."

"One of those things should be 'I'm sorry,'" Brendan puts in pointedly.

She glares at him. "We'll see. But if it is, it'll be the last item on my list."

"Where *is* Chase?" Kimberly asks in annoyance. "Brendan, you said he was going to be here."

Brendan is already on his phone, talking with Mrs. Ambrose. He frowns, thanks her, and hangs up. "According to his mom, he's on his way to Portland Street. She said he was in a real hurry."

"Did he forget to come?" I ask.

Brendan shakes his head. "He said he'd be here. He just texted a couple of hours ago."

Shosh stands up. "Let's go over to Portland Street."

CHAPTER TWENTY-SEVEN

AARON HAKIMIAN

"Young man, we've been waiting nearly half an hour," the Dumbledora tells me. "You promised to set up the card table for us."

"We'll get to it," I tell her. "We're busy."

This old bat has a voice like screeching gears on a truck with a bad transmission. "You don't look very busy to me. You're just standing around the snack cart eating the cookies you're supposed to be passing out."

"Which is a big job." Bear pretends to be outraged. "You expect us to do it on an empty stomach?"

"Chill out," I advise Dumbledora. "Five more minutes."

It goes without saying that community service at the Graybeard Motel is about as much fun as sticking your hand in a garbage disposal. The one good thing is you get to mess with the residents. She's been bugging us half the morning to set up an extra card table in the rec room so she and three other blue-hairs can play bridge. We've been having a few laughs seeing how long we can blow her off. Five minutes? Try five hours. Maybe five days. If she doesn't like it, let her set up her own card table. She's built like a sumo wrestler.

In frustration, she retreats into the rec room and Bear and I crack up. Oh, we'll do it for her eventually—you know, right before her head explodes. That's the art to it—picking the moment to give in just when she's about to report us to the nurses.

We help ourselves to more cookies, but Bear tries to hog the last chocolate one and we end up down on the floor, fighting for it and laughing like crazy. The cookie is crushed before either of us can eat it.

We're getting back to our feet, brushing off the dust and crumbs, when we see him: Chase, striding down the hall like he's on *The Amazing Race*—in a real hurry to get somewhere, and not too thrilled about it. Ever since our fight on the football field, he hasn't been turning up for community service—not that he's really on it, anyway. I guess he's back—or at least he's back visiting his video star, the nastiest old Dumbledore in a building overflowing with them.

Bear, who has amazing sight, spots the bulging pocket first. It looks like he's carrying a baseball, but there's a piece of cloth trailing from the opening.

"Hey, Ambrose," I call. "What've you got there?"

He ignores me and shifts his path to the opposite side of the corridor.

Bear blocks his way. "The man asked you a question."

Another shift, so I step out beside Bear, and together we block the hall. Chase does exactly what a running back would do on a football field: He puts his head down and tries to blast through us. But we're linemen, and we stop him cold. In a game, I'd be trying to strip the ball. In this case, I reach down, grab the white fabric, and yank.

A dish towel opens up in my hand, and something flies out of it and hits the terrazzo floor with a clink. Star shape, blue ribbon—the geezer's medal. Chase falls on it like he's recovering a fumble. Bear and I go down on top of him.

"Two-thirds of that is ours!" I snarl.

"It belongs to Mr. Solway!"

"He doesn't care!" Bear grunts. "He barely remembers he ever had it!"

"Get *off*!"

Somehow, he heaves us both clear and scrambles to his feet, clutching the medal in his hand.

"You're not going to win this, man," I tell him. It's not even unfriendly; I'm giving him valuable information. "We're taking that medal no matter what we have to do to you."

He hesitates, considering his options. During the pause, Dumbledora comes back into the hall. "What's going on out here? It's more than five minutes. We need our table set up. Now."

"Oh, I'll do it," offers Chase, grabbing the opportunity to get away from us.

The medal concealed in his fist, he escorts Dumbledora into the rec room. Bear starts to follow them, but I hold him back. "Too many witnesses, man. Be patient. He can't stay in there forever."

We watch like hawks from the doorway, figuring he might try to stash the medal and come back for it later, when we're not around. It's in his right hand. He never opens those fingers while he's setting up the folding table and chairs. He keeps one eye on us. I favor him with a grin that says: *We're going to get you if we have to stand here until the next ice age.*

"He's toast," Bear whispers triumphantly. "The only way out of the room is through us."

The Dumbledoras in the rec room are fawning over Ambrose like he just saved the world from Lex Luthor or something. They love him as much as they hate us. It's enough to make you barf. He even takes a small potted plant from the TV cabinet and sets it on the table to be a centerpiece. The bluehairs are practically wriggling with joy.

Then, as Chase turns, his elbow knocks the pot off the table. It hits the floor and shatters, spilling earth all over the place.

Bear loves it. "Ha! Idiot!"

Ambrose rushes to the corner, where a vacuum cleaner stands against the wall. He plugs it in and starts to clean up his mess.

We almost miss it. As he runs the vacuum back and forth over the dirt, he opens his hand and drops the medal into the unit's path. In a heartbeat, it's sucked up and gone. He glances over his shoulder to see if we noticed. I pretend we didn't, but Bear's face is bright red, which is a dead giveaway.

Chase is vacuuming toward us now, speeding up, breaking into a run. The plug pops out of the wall. The vacuum falls silent. He keeps moving, though, charging at us. Bear and I block the doorway and brace ourselves to deck him again. Just before impact, he lifts the vacuum cleaner like a battering ram and slams into us.

We're both knocked back onto our butts, choking in a cloud of dust that the collision forces out of the filter bag. By the time our vision clears and we struggle back up again, Ambrose is almost of out sight down the hall, still cradling the vacuum cleaner.

We stare at each other, and the minute we get our breath back, we chorus, "Get him!"

We take off after our star running back. We've never been able to outpace him before. But this time, he's carrying a vacuum cleaner, not a football.

That's bound to slow him down.

CHAPTER TWENTY-EIGHT

SHOSHANNA WEBER

By the time I get to Portland Street, I'm walking so fast that the others are half a block behind me and running to catch up.

Chase! I didn't think I could be madder at him than I already am. But this almost makes it worse. He's innocent of the attack on Joel—I saw it with my own eyes.

It was easier when I could just hate his guts, no questions asked. But it's not as simple as that. Now, every time I work myself into a good rage, I'll see him trying to protect Joel, or working with the video club, or interacting with Mr. Solway. And that will ruin everything. It's the mix of good and bad that makes my head spin.

Worse, a lot of the mean things I said turn out to be wrong, and it might be too late to take them back.

In the lobby, I wait for the others to catch up and drag them down the hall to Mr. Solway's room. I knock on the door, but burst inside without waiting for an answer. The old man is doubled over in his favorite chair, working at his sneaker lace with intense concentration. Spying me, he exclaims, "Well, don't just stand there. Come on in and help me undo this knot. I don't bend in the middle like I used to. And when I do get close enough, I can't see it!"

I step inside and the others follow.

"By all means," Mr. Solway adds, "invite the whole world. Watch the old codger trying to untie his shoes. Who's bringing the popcorn? You're going to have to blow up the balloons yourselves. I haven't got the wind for it anymore."

I kneel down and pick the knot out of his shoelace. "Mr. Solway," I ask breathlessly, "has Chase been here yet?"

He shakes his head. "Haven't seen him in days. You either," he adds, a little accusingly.

I feel awful. I haven't come by since Joel got hurt. And now I realize that Chase hasn't visited since that horrible day either. It never occurred to me before because my only thoughts about Chase were how much I despised him. But to Mr. Solway it must look like we didn't need him anymore because our video was finished. And we just tossed him aside.

"It's my fault," I confess. "I got mad at Chase for something that was only partly his fault. That's why he stopped coming. Not because he didn't want to see you, but because he didn't want to see *me*. And I stopped because I didn't want to run into *him* . . ."

I feel a hand on my shoulder. Joel is standing next to me and I realize that he's trying to tell me I'm getting so worked up about this emotionally that I'm not making much sense.

A crooked smile spreads over Mr. Solway's craggy face. "I wouldn't be young again for all the tea in China."

Kimberly steps forward. "We saw a movie about you in my school."

"That was *Warrior*," Brendan supplies quickly. "The project Shoshanna and Chase did together."

There's a commotion out in the hall—loud voices and pounding footsteps.

Mr. Solway frowns. "Not wheelchair Roller Derby again. The Greatest Generation—they think they own the world!"

I poke my head out the door in time to see Chase sprinting toward me with, of all things, a vacuum cleaner clutched in his arms. As I watch, he's yanked violently backward off his feet. He falls hard, still clinging to the appliance. Aaron is on the floor behind him, both hands on the electrical cord that brought Chase down.

Bear hurdles the fallen Aaron and descends on Chase like a bird of prey. And when Chase won't give up the vacuum, Bear rains punches on his head and shoulders.

I hear a cry of outrage from Kimberly, but it's not as loud as my own. The two of us rush forward and jump on Bear, trying to pull him off Chase. And it works. He scrambles back to his feet and shoves us away from him. Kimberly bounces off the wall, and as we stumble together, our heads meet with a crack. I see stars.

"Hey!" Little undersized Brendan comes flying at Bear, his anger lending him courage nobody ever knew he had. He begins pummeling Bear, landing blow after blow. It's insane—David versus Goliath. He isn't even making proper fists—his thumbs stick out like apple stems.

Then Bear's shocked expression turns to cruel glee and he

laughs even as Brendan continues to flail at him. Finally, he hauls off and catches his much smaller assailant with a bone-crushing uppercut to the jaw. Brendan lifts off the floor and lands six feet away.

Amazingly, Brendan gets up, his chin bright red from the punch, and starts for Bear again.

Chase is on his feet, reaching out to hold Brendan off. It's a good idea. Those two gorillas could really dismantle him. Aaron snatches the vacuum off the floor and draws it back like a baseball bat—and the ball is Chase's head.

I rasp a warning. "Chase—!"

Mr. Solway's walker comes freewheeling down the hall. It slams into Aaron's kidneys just when he's off balance for the home-run swing. He and the vacuum tip over backward onto Bear. Three of them—Aaron, Bear, and the Hoover—clatter to the floor.

"Ha—bull's-eye!" exclaims Mr. Solway with satisfaction.

"There they are!"

The heavy doors at the end of the corridor are thrown open, and Joel appears, leading Nurse Duncan and two security guards.

Way to go, Joel! At least somebody had the brains to go for help.

Aaron and Bear are ready to fight another round, but the arrival of security and the head nurse puts an end to the action. Brawling in the middle of court-ordered community service won't look good on their records.

Bear points an accusing finger at Chase. "It's *his* fault!"

Nurse Duncan is in a towering rage. "*What* is?" Residents are beginning to appear in doorways to investigate the cause of the disturbance, so the head nurse drops her voice. "What is all this *insanity* about?"

In answer, Chase pulls the filter bag off the Hoover and dumps the contents onto the floor. He digs through the mound of fuzz and dirt and comes up with a star-spangled ribbon, gray with dust. Dangling off the end of it is the highest and most renowned military decoration any American soldier can earn. The Medal of Honor—not even the contents of the vacuum bag can dull its brilliance.

"Is that mine?" Mr. Solway asks in amazement.

Chase nods. "I took it from you. I don't remember doing it—it was before my accident. But that's no excuse." He hands it to its rightful owner and bows his head, shamefaced.

"It was the old you!" Brendan mumbles around a rapidly swelling jaw.

"There's only one me." Chase says it so quietly that I can hardly hear him.

Mr. Solway turns the medal over in his fingers. He seems stunned. "What about those two clowns?" he asks. "Were they in on it?"

Aaron and Bear turn terrified eyes on their former best friend.

"It was just me," Chase replies. "I took it and I hid it behind a loose cedar shake on the roof of my house. That's what I was doing when I fell. I guess I got what I deserved." He shakes his head. "I don't know why I would do such an awful thing. I must have thought I could sell it."

Mr. Solway looks shocked and very sad.

I almost speak up for Chase, but the sight of the stolen medal strikes me mute. Good Chase, bad Chase—there's no question that we're looking at the handiwork of the worst one of all.

I can tell that Joel wants to support Chase, but he doesn't know what to say. He's the quiet twin; I'm the mouthy one. Brendan's jaw is turning purple, so he's not talking either. Kimberly's completely lost. And Aaron and Bear are so relieved that no one's blaming them that they're keeping their mouths shut too.

The only words come from Nurse Duncan. "Well, I have no idea what any of this is supposed to mean. The one thing I understand is that a crime has been committed here." She takes a deep breath. "I'm calling the police."

CHAPTER TWENTY-NINE

CHASE AMBROSE

There are worse things than falling off a roof.

Being arrested, for example. Being known all over town as the guy who was low enough to rob an old war hero of the medal given to him by the president of the United States.

The part that really hurts is what Mr. Solway must think of me now. I stole from the person I respect more than anybody I've ever met. Talk about fate! I was already guilty of the theft before I even started admiring the guy. And I'm absolutely sure he'll never speak to me again. Why should he? I wish *I* could never speak to me again.

While we wait for my hearing in juvenile court, Mom keeps me out of school. I like it better that way. I don't have to face everybody and find out how much they despise me. Yeah, sure, they always despised me. But now they've got double reason to. Brendan and Shoshanna have even called my house, but Mom won't let me talk to anyone. That's on the advice of our lawyer, but it's just fine with me. I can only imagine what Shoshanna has to say to me, and I don't want to hear it. Anyway, it can't be worse than the things I'm saying to myself.

Aaron and Bear tried to call too—probably to thank me for covering for them. Hey, *I* stole the medal, but those guys have to be considered at least accomplices, because of our three-way-split agreement. To be honest, I'm not even that mad at them anymore. I was just as bad as they are, the ringleader of the whole sick trio. They haven't changed at all. I'm the one who's different.

At least I hope I'm different.

Besides, I won't have to deal with them anymore after the hearing. I'll probably wind up in juvie. Even when I get out, chances are their parents won't let them associate with me. I'm a delinquent, a bad influence on them. For all I know, that might actually be the truth. Maybe Aaron and Bear were a couple of angels before they met me.

Juvie—there's a really high probability I'm going to end up there. The judge is the same one who sentenced Aaron, Bear, and me to community service, so I can't even say this is my first offense. As for pleading not guilty—it's too late for that. Everybody knows I did it.

My mom forgives me, but that doesn't mean much. If you can't expect mercy from your own mother, you might as well throw in the towel. Johnny's come back from college to stand with me at the hearing, which means I'm messing up *his* life too.

The only other people I ever see are Dad and his family. Go figure, my stepmother, Corinne, turns out to be my biggest fan at a time when I'm toe jam to the rest of the world. Not that Mom isn't supportive, but she's so scared of what's going to happen to me that her nervousness is making everybody nuts.

Corinne's different. First, I'm not her kid. And second, she's not the one who might be going to juvie. So she can be a little less emotional about all this. "I have to believe that the judge will be able to see the kind of person you are."

"I guess I was pretty rotten to you and Helene," I say. "You know—before. I don't remember it, but I'm still sorry."

"Never mind that," she replies. "Let's focus on how things are now."

Helene is only four, so she understands nothing about my problems. Actually, the only time I feel really relaxed these days is when I'm sitting on the floor with her, playing Barbies—something the old Chase wouldn't have been caught dead doing.

I'm pushing Malibu Barbie's beach cruiser, giving Ken a ride to the luau, when I notice Dad filming me on his phone.

"I thought playing with a four-year-old interferes with your focus on important things, like football," I tell him.

"Are you kidding, Champ?" he exclaims. "We can show this at your trial—"

"It's a hearing."

"Whatever. It'll prove to the judge what a great big brother you are. And that will get you *back* on the football field."

I sigh. "I guess you think I'm a pretty big moron for returning that medal."

He actually seems to mull it over. "Well, I'd be lying if I didn't say it would have been a lot smarter just to slip it under Solway's door."

"Yeah, tell me about it."

"But you did the right thing," he adds. "That medal's worthless to you. You didn't earn it—not like your state championship, let's say. It only has value to Mr. Solway."

"I don't know how valuable it is to him either. He can't remember any of what he did to win it. He blanked it out the way I blanked out my whole past."

Dad shrugs. "Even if you can't remember it, it still happened. I loved the kid you used to be—"

I start to protest, and he holds up a hand. "Let me finish. Just because I miss the old Chase doesn't mean I don't appreciate who you are now. I'm not blind. I see the bond you have with Helene. You think that would have been possible before your accident?"

"I thought you considered that kind of stuff weakness."

He reddens. "I just didn't know the new you yet. It takes *strength* to eat the blame and not rat out Aaron and Bear, especially when they more than deserve it. Or to try to make things right with Solway or even the Weber kid, whether they appreciate it or not. You're strong, all right. And stupid. But everybody has stupid moments. The trick is not to let a few bad moments cost you the game."

There's something in his expression that I've never noticed before. It was probably there a lot before the accident, but this is the first time that I actually see it.

Pride.

Which is going to be worth exactly zero in front of a judge.

As I step through the metal detector at the courthouse, I freeze. I've been here before, and the memory comes flooding back.

"Move it along, son," the security guard urges me. "Plenty of people in line behind you."

"Right—sorry." I stumble forward to make room for Mom, Johnny, Dad, and Mr. Landau, our lawyer.

I must look a little shaky, because my brother whispers, "Hang in there, kid."

I nod, wrapped up in my latest flashback—arriving in this very building with Aaron, Bear, and our families. What I remember the most is my anger, my outrage that the three of us were being hauled into court for booby-trapping Joel's piano. I was mad at everybody—Joel, the Webers, the school, the police. Didn't they know who I was? Chase Ambrose, MVP of the state championship game! We *ruled* that school—whatever we did was okay just because it was us who did it! Yeah, I was mad. I can practically feel the heat of my rage radiating through the memory.

What a difference a few months make. Back then I had such a high opinion of the great Chase Ambrose that I considered myself untouchable. Now it's the opposite. I hate myself so much that there's no way any judge could hate me more. That's why Mr. Landau has been so frustrated with me. How can you create a defense for someone who won't defend himself?

It's not that I *want* to get sent to juvie. I don't. But I'm one hundred percent guilty. I took the medal; I hid the medal; and if I'd been my old self, I would have sold the medal and pocketed the money. There it is, my whole case. That's probably why Mr. Landau's betting everything on character witnesses. Because I refuse to say anything on my own behalf.

I hear my mom drawing a tremulous breath as we enter the courtroom. My dad puts an arm around my shoulders. Believe it or not, I don't even shrug it off. Right now, I need all the support I can get.

When I take my first look around, I almost lose it.

Everybody's here!

Brendan and Kimmy are sitting with the video club, along with a lot of kids from school. I see Coach Davenport and a group of football players—Joey and Landon and some others. Ms. DeLeo is there too, along with several of my teachers. In the front row, I'm shocked to find Shoshanna, Joel, and their parents. Shoshanna catches me looking at her and quickly turns her head.

I'm blown away. I already know I'm not the most popular guy in Hiawassee. But the fact that so many people despise me so much that they'd take time out of their day to come and watch me get sentenced to juvie is the most painful thing I've ever had to face. All that's missing is the stocks so the angry mob can throw rotten vegetables at me.

Judge Garfinkle comes in and spends a few minutes reviewing the case file while I sit there and stew. "Oh, I remember now." He turns his sharp gaze on me. "Young man, I told you that if I ever saw you in my courtroom again, things would go very hard with you. What do you have to say for yourself?"

Mr. Landau starts to get up, and while he's buttoning his jacket, I reply, "Nothing, Your Honor. I don't remember why I stole Mr. Solway's medal. I wouldn't do it today. But I definitely did it then."

The judge nods gravely. "I appreciate your honesty. You're making my job easier, if not any more pleasant."

"I have some character witnesses who would like to be heard," Mr. Landau announces, "if it pleases the court."

Judge Garfinkle sighs. "Proceed."

Mom goes first, dripping enough tears to warp the wood of the witness stand. Her main message is what a difficult child I used to be and how much I've changed since my accident. She spends a lot of time talking about how seriously injured I was and how long I was unconscious. This comes from Mr. Landau's careful coaching, but Judge Garfinkle looks about as easy to persuade as one of those giant stone heads on Easter Island.

Dad is next, and I'm amazed at some of the things he says. I thought all he cared about was that I'm a chip off the old block. But he only mentions football once. "What kid doesn't act like he's got it all figured out when he's Chase's age? Even so, getting to know my son the way he is now, I almost wish someone had pushed me off a roof when I was thirteen."

I'm stunned. The very best part of my father's forty-eight years was the time he spent in middle and high school. He considers himself to have been the ultimate athlete, hotshot, and big man on campus. He has never—not once—allowed for even the remotest possibility that his youth was anything less than perfect. Until today, when he thought it might help me.

Dr. Cooperman comes up to confirm that my head trauma was as serious as we say it was. Enough to bring on amnesia, and enough to cause a personality change.

Judge Garfinkle frowns. "And the personality change is permanent?"

"It's impossible to tell," the doctor admits. "In many ways, we know more about outer space than we do about the innermost workings of the human brain. But there's every reason to believe that Chase is a new person."

As Dr. Cooperman steps down, the bailiff reads the name of the next character witness.

"Shoshanna Weber."

What? I'm frozen in my chair. That has to be a mistake! But no—Shoshanna has gotten up and is heading to the stand.

I tug on Mr. Landau's sleeve. "No!" I hiss. This "character witness" thinks I'm subhuman garbage!

She's still avoiding eye contact with me, but there's an intense expression on her face. She's a girl on a mission. And I know exactly what the mission is—to bury me. She doesn't say anything, just sits there, steam building inside her like a boiler about to explode.

Not good. Oh, this is *so* not good!

"Miss Weber?" prompts the judge.

"I know Chase is guilty," she begins. "He's guilty of a lot of things. But he's done a lot of good things too. He's *trying*—even if he isn't always succeeding."

Judge Garfinkle clears his throat. "Young lady, the purpose of a character witness is to vouch for character, not to point out faults."

"I was getting to that part," she tells him. "The big question is, what kind of person is Chase going to be now? He gave the medal back—that's a plus. But there are minuses too, like at school, when he lied to cover up for his old friends. I'm not saying that to make him look bad; I'm trying to give you a totally fair picture of Chase today. Thanks to falling off that roof, he's been given a chance to restart his whole life. Maybe it hasn't been perfect . . ." She struggles for the right words.

I'm silently pulling for her not to find them. I'm grateful that she doesn't seem to hate me as much as before, but *this isn't helping*!

"And . . . ?" the judge prods.

"I was harder on Chase than anybody else," she explains. "And some of that was justified and some of it wasn't. I guess what I mean is, if *I* have faith that he's going to turn out okay, you can take it to the bank. And I'm amazed to say this, but I just *know* he'll be a good person."

Huh?

It wasn't the kind of testimonial Mr. Landau was hoping for, but it was absolutely honest. For sure, I wasn't expecting to hear the words *good person* coming from Shoshanna—not when she was talking about me.

Don't get me wrong. If the Webers forgive me, that would be a humongous weight lifted off my shoulders. Mostly, though, I'm just confused. This isn't going at all the way I expected.

"That's admirable of you to say, Miss Weber," Judge Garfinkle comments from the bench. "But that isn't what this hearing is about. Chase is charged with the theft of a Medal of Honor belonging to Mr. Julius Solway—which nobody denies happened, not even Chase himself."

"But don't you see?" she pleads. "If I can misjudge him, anybody can. Even a judge."

"Thank you for your testimony," he tells Shoshanna. "Let's move along. Would anybody else here like to say something on behalf of this young man?"

The chorus of squeaking chair backs and shuffling feet is louder than it should be. That's when I realize that *every single person in the gallery* has gotten up. They cross the courtroom in the direction of the witness stand—kids, teachers, and parents alike. The only occupied seats belong to my family and Mr. Landau. Everybody else is in line in front of the bewildered bailiff. Video club kids I know I pushed around in the past. Teachers whose classes I used to disrupt. Football players who thought I deserted them. Even Joel and his parents.

I stare at them—practically everyone I know, waiting their turn to support the bully who deserves no support at all. They nod encouragingly at me, wave, flash me thumbs-up. The picture doesn't last long. My eyes fill with tears, and it's all a blur. I was afraid I might cry at some point during the hearing. But not because of this. This is something I couldn't have imagined in a million centuries.

I bite down on the side of my mouth—hard—and my vision clears a little.

From the bench, Judge Garfinkle gazes at the milling crowd. "All right, I get it." He turns to me. "This is impressive, and I don't deny that you must have completed an incredible turnaround. But a serious crime has been committed here—and not a first offense either. Chase, can you guarantee that you're no longer the same person who stole Mr. Solway's medal?"

I sense salvation so close I can almost reach out and squeeze it. All I have to do is say yes and I'm off the hook. It's a happier ending than I could have dreamed of, far happier than I have any right to expect. And yet—

How do I know I'm one hundred percent different? As the memories continue to trickle back, it's pretty clear that the old me and the new me aren't two separate Chases. Can I really claim to be "no longer the same person"?

Of course, that wouldn't stop me from telling the judge what he wants to hear. It's what the old Chase would do—take the easy way out, like that time in Dr. Fitzwallace's office. Lie, cheat, say anything to beat the rap.

I'd be proving that I haven't changed a bit. Okay, Judge Garfinkle will never know the difference.

But *I* will.

And in that instant, I understand that being true to myself is more important than fooling the judge with the power to send me to juvie.

I shake my head sadly. "I'm sorry, Your Honor, but I can't make that guarantee. I *feel* different; I have no urge to do the things I used to do. But the person who stole the medal was inside me once. I can't promise that he's gone forever."

There's almost a wind in the courtroom—all those people deflating at the same time. Shoshanna. Joel. Brendan. My parents.

Judge Garfinkle lets out a heavy breath. "In that case,

Chase Ambrose, you've left me no choice. It is the decision of this court that you be remanded to the juvenile authorities—"

"Now, hold on just one cotton-pickin' minute!"

In the excitement, nobody's noticed that the courtroom doors have been flung wide. In shuffles Mr. Julius Solway, war hero, struggling behind his walker. Around the neck of his one and only suit hangs his Medal of Honor, freshly polished and gleaming. The look in his blazing eyes plainly says he intends to take on the world—and win.

That gets the judge's attention. "I assume I'm addressing Mr. Solway. Please take a seat, sir."

"No, I'm not going to take a seat," Mr. Solway replies belligerently. "All this ruckus over a stupid medal! Well, here it is with its rightful owner. Case closed. Now, let's all go home. It's taco night at Portland Street."

The judge is respectful but firm. "It doesn't work that way, Mr. Solway. A crime has been committed here, even if it now has a satisfactory ending."

"What crime?" Mr. Solway challenges. "Chase didn't steal my medal. I loaned it to him."

I jump up. "Mr. Solway, don't—"

"What do you know about it?" the old soldier roars at me. "You fell on your head and lost your memory. Who are you going to believe, Judge? The fellow who remembers or the fellow who doesn't?"

Judge Garfinkle frowns. "This may be juvenile court, but it's still a court of law. We deal in the truth and only the truth."

"The truth is this is a good kid. How many people do you have to hear it from?" Mr. Solway indicates the lineup in front of the witness stand. "I'd trust him with my medal anytime. Why wouldn't I?"

Mr. Landau steps forward eagerly. "I believe Mr. Solway has introduced—reasonable doubt."

The judge snorts a laugh at him. "Watch it, counsel. I'm not an idiot." His harsh expression softens. "However, in light of the incredible show of community support, plus the testimony of a decorated veteran, I'm going to dismiss the charge against Chase Ambrose." He looks me straight in the eye. "Don't prove me wrong."

I breathe, and realize breathing is something I haven't been doing since Mr. Solway came shuffling through that door.

An enormous cheer goes up in the courtroom. I'm hugged, kissed, and high-fived; my hand is pumped to the point where my elbow is jelly; my back is pounded until Dr. Cooperman warns about internal injuries. The football players carry me around on their shoulders. Coach Davenport complains that he hasn't seen this much team spirit all season.

There, high above my celebrating supporters, I experience another flashback. It's the state championship from last season, and this is our on-field victory dance, my teammates hoisting the newly crowned MVP up in the air. I slap myself in the face to dispel the memory before I spot Aaron or Bear and spoil it.

I'm feeling so many things at the same time. I'm relieved,

obviously. But it's also strange to owe so many people such a debt of gratitude. Back on the floor, I say thank you over and over again until my lips and tongue go numb. And when the crowd finally begins to thin out, I realize that the last person embracing me isn't my mother; it's Shoshanna. We jump apart, but Joel is already standing there, pointing and laughing.

"I guess he's not going in the wood chipper after all," he says to his sister.

I look at her questioningly. She turns bright red and mumbles, "See you at school tomorrow." She starts to walk away, then turns and echoes Judge Garfinkle's parting words. "Chase—don't prove me wrong."

Come to think of it, Shoshanna would make a pretty good judge. She'd make an even better jury and executioner.

I wouldn't want her any other way.

When the Webers leave, I'm down to my last thank-you, and this one's the most important.

Mr. Solway has established himself in the front row of the gallery. He's scowling at me. "You know, kid, you'd make a lousy lawyer. You almost blew it up there."

"Mr. Solway, you know you didn't lend me that medal."

He shrugs expansively. "I would have. Besides, you have amnesia; I'm old. Who remembers? But think where you'd be if I hadn't been able to get a lift over here."

"Thank you so much!" I quaver, thinking about how hard it is for him to get around.

"Don't thank me. Thank *her*."

He motions to the back of the courtroom. There, by the

door, stands Corinne. One hand holds on to Helene, the other to the keys of her van. She's beaming at me.

It's funny. When I woke up in the hospital at the end of the summer, I didn't even know myself, much less anybody else. I hope I never again experience a feeling that lonely. But today, with my entire future at stake, I wasn't alone.

The Chase Ambrose I used to be never would have assembled such support. Mom and Dad. Johnny. Probably Aaron and Bear, who have to be worse than nobody as character witnesses. Maybe a few more teammates, out of obligation. That would have been the sum total of my cheering section.

I follow my family out onto the steps of the courthouse and take a tremulous lungful of free air.

How many people ever get a do-over at life?

Falling on my head was the best thing that ever happened to me.

CHAPTER THIRTY

BRENDAN ESPINOZA

It has to be the most incredible transformation in the history of middle school.

No, not Chase Ambrose going from thug bully sociopath to human being—although surely that's in the top ten.

I'm talking about the fact that Kimberly likes me now.

I swear, I'm black-and-blue from pinching myself to make sure I'm not dreaming. But it's one hundred percent legit. I even call her Kimmy. It's like a pet name. Nobody else calls her that. If that's not the real thing, I don't know what is.

It was the big fight at Portland Street that did it. When Kimmy saw me sacrificing myself—and getting the snot knocked out of me—trying to protect her from Aaron and Bear, that put it over the top. I was like a knight in shining armor—although Kimmy says it's mostly because she was so amazed I wasn't dead. Whatever. Before this, she had trouble remembering my name.

Anyway, a bruised jaw is a small price to pay for a girlfriend—especially the most mad-awesome one in all of Hiawassee.

I'm not even worried that she might go back to her old crush on Chase. It looks like Chase and Shoshanna might be starting to turn into something. Not that I'm planning double dates with them anytime soon. No sense playing with fire.

Chase played his first football game of the season last weekend, and really tore it up, scoring three touchdowns and gaining a hundred and eighty yards. Shoshanna annoyed the crowd by standing in the middle of the bleachers and delivering a long speech about how she isn't a football fan and never intends to become one. Maybe, maybe not. After all, people change. Look at Chase himself. Or Kimmy. Or the video club. We know less than zero about football, but we got some amazing footage of that game. Coach Davenport liked it so much that he made us the Hurricanes' official videographers. The pep band has a new student musical director too—Joel Weber.

The players are kind of nice to us now—well, most of them anyway. Aaron and Bear are still their usual Neanderthal selves. Then again, everything that happened pretty much exposed those two as the bullies and delinquents they are. Who cares about them? They're kind of outcasts. Chase says even the other Hurricanes pretty much ignore them. Not that those two being losers was ever a news flash to me.

Chase is back in the video club where he belongs. In fact, he's a bigger star there than in football. The word just came in that *Warrior* took first prize in the National Video Journalism Contest. Chase is the sole winner since Shoshanna removed her name from the project when she thought he attacked Joel. Ms. DeLeo is trying to get that fixed.

The vidiots have adopted Mr. Solway as our official

mascot. We wanted to make him our official war hero, but he objects to the word *hero.* He's not too crazy about *war* either.

Well, he may not let us call him *our* hero, but he's definitely *my* hero because of what he did in court for Chase that day. But of course, he was a hero long before any of us was born. The United States Army was so convinced of it that they awarded him their very highest honor.

Just don't try to ask him about it.

"I can't remember anything, kid, so don't bug me," he barks in his best crabby old man voice. "Talk to Chase—he'll tell you what it's like to blank something out."

Actually, Chase is recalling more and more these days. He's still got a long way to go before his amnesia is totally cured. But every now and then, I'll see him in the school halls, gray in the face and haunted, and I know he's just remembered some horrible thing he did in his former life. Poor guy. Maybe one day he'll get used to it, and it won't bother him so much. But I'm not holding my breath.

I always thought the purpose of video club was to create something so off the chain that it goes viral and makes you famous. But that's not the point at all. The best thing about video club is the people you discover along the way. Like Mr. Solway. Or Kimmy, who probably never would have noticed me otherwise. Or Chase, who I spent three-quarters of my life being afraid of, and is now one of my best friends.

Which doesn't mean that you have to give up on the viral part. Kimmy took my raw footage from *One Man Band* and edited out everything except the part where I'm trapped in the tuba, being shot with fire extinguisher foam. Then she posted it to YouTube under the title *Worst Tuba Fail Ever* and it's already been viewed 360,000 times!

Unbelievable! *I* have a viral video! Well, technically, it's Kimmy's video, since she posted it on her own account and never mentioned my name, not even once. I'm just the doofus in the tuba, wriggling like a hula dancer and foaming at the mouth. But it still counts.

It proves *anything* is possible.

Kimmy and me.

A YouTube sensation.

Even Chase Ambrose turning out to be a nice guy.

ABOUT THE AUTHOR

Gordon Korman is the #1 bestselling author of four books in The 39 Clues series as well as eight books in his Swindle series: *Swindle*, *Zoobreak*, *Framed*, *Showoff*, *Hideout*, *Jackpot*, *Unleashed*, and *Jingle*. His other books include *This Can't Be Happening at Macdonald Hall!* (published when he was fourteen); *The Toilet Paper Tigers*; *Radio Fifth Grade*; *Ungifted*; *Schooled*; *Slacker*; the trilogies Island, Everest, Dive, Kidnapped, Titanic, and The Hypnotists; and the series On the Run. He lives in New York with his family and can be found on the Web at www.gordonkorman.com.